MYSTERY

—— BOOK 2 ——

Shawn Pierce

PAGE PUBLISHING, INC.
New York, NY

First originally published by Page Publishing, Inc. 2017

ISBN 978-1-64082-684-7 (Paperback)
ISBN 978-1-64082-685-4 (Digital)

Printed in the United States of America

PART 4

Episode 1

Armon walked back to his hotel. On his way there, he started remembering the good times he had with Alexandria and Jase. He realized what he did to her almost a year ago was wrong, and it was all because he had a drinking problem. Even though he wasn't drinking anymore due to that, Alexandria would never believe it and he knew it. He would have to take the time to show her every chance he got.

His first issue he needed to deal with was Jase and convincing him that he was not this bad person that Max made him out to be. Armon and Jase were really close, and it hurt Armon to know that his son wanted nothing to do with him.

Armon: (To himself.) That's okay. Max better come through for me. If he doesn't, I swear I will tell Adriana the truth about him.

MALIK'S HOUSE

Malena: Ivy, you scared me.

Ivy: I'm sure. You weren't expecting me to overhear you.

Malena picked the phone up off the floor and hung it up. Max was still on the other line.

Malena: I don't know what you think you heard.

Ivy: Don't play with me. I know exactly what I heard. You said Malik is not Ashley's father. Is that true?

Malena: I said nothing of the sort.

Ivy: Okay, you want to play dumb with me. How about I just call Malik right now?

Ivy went to dial on her cell phone.

Malena: Ivy, don't, please.

Ivy: Then tell me the truth because I know what I heard.

Malena: Okay, yes, it's true.

Malena started to cry.

Malena: Ivy, I know Malik is your brother, but you can't tell him. He will never understand why I kept this from him.

Ivy: Are you kidding me? He has every right to know. How could you keep this from him? All the sacrifices he has made over the years to keep you happy and you do this to him. Of course I'm going to tell him.

Ivy started to walk off, but Malena grabbed her by the arm.

Malena: Ivy, please, don't do this. I love him and I don't was to lose my family. I'm begging you, please.

Ivy: You should have thought about that before you slept with another man.

Ivy: (Snatching her arm away.) Let go of me.

She headed for the door. Malena was right behind her pleading. All of a sudden, Malena panic. Before Ivy could make it to the door, Malena picked up a vase and hit Ivy over the head with it, breaking the vase into pieces. Ivy fell to the floor unconscious.

AT THE HOSPITAL

Dr. Baker: Diane, wait a minute. Are you sure, absolutely positive that either Kennedy or Jackson is the father?

Diane: (Getting angry.) Of course, I'm sure. You think I would make something like this up?

Dr. Baker: No, I'm not saying that.

Diane: (*Very snappy.*) Then what are you saying?

Dr. Baker: I just want you to be certain. That's all.

Diane: Well, I am. I always knew when and where my boys were conceived—now that, I am certain of. I just never thought I would ever see the guys again, let alone be dating one of their best friends.

The doctor got up out his chair and came around in front of his desk. He sat down in the chair next to Diane.

Dr. Baker: Diane, what are you going to do? What do you want to do?

On the next episode, Diane makes her decision.

Episode 2

Dr. Baker: Diane, what are you going to do? What do you want to do?

Diane: I don't know. (She stands up.) I need to think about this for a minute. Part of me is saying to just leave it alone and another part is telling me to find out.

Dr. Baker: You need to decide. Either way, people's lives will be impacted by this. If you decide not to find out who the father is, then you will constantly be living a lie not telling your sons. If you do decide to find out, people's lives will change.

Diane: I know. I know. What should I do?

Dr. Baker: I can't decide that for you. That is a decision you will have to make. I can only speak of what I would do in a situation like this.

Diane: And what is that? Tell me.

Dr. Baker: I would definitely want to know. (The doctor stands up.) There is no rush. Why don't you take the time to think about it?

Diane: (Thinking for a minute.) No, I need to know. I need to know who the father is.

MALIK'S HOUSE

Malena just stood there with her hands over her mouth. She couldn't believe what she had done. She looked upstairs to make sure Melanie and Ashley didn't hear her. Malena then kneeled down beside Ivy to see if she had a pulse.

Malena: Thank God there's a pulse.

(She stands up to collect herself.) Basement. (Whispering to herself.) She realized that they had a room down there that they never used, only for storage.

Malena turned Ivy over. By her arms, she dragged Ivy across the living room floor and through the kitchen. When she made it to the basement door, she dropped Ivy's arms to catch her breath.

Ashley called out from upstairs. "Mom?"

Malena got nervous. She yelled back, "Stay there, Ashley. I'm coming."

Malena opened the basement door and proceeded to drag Ivy down the stairs. She dragged her over to the storage room and unlocked the door. They always kept the key itself in the lock. The storage room was full of boxes taped up, old clothes hanging up, and old toys. She got a chair that was stored in there and sat it up. She dragged Ivy into the storage room and put her in the chair. Malena found some duct-tape. She taped Ivy's ankles to the chair legs and taped her arms to the arms of the chair. She then put tape across her mouth. Ivy was still unconscious. Malena stack some boxes in front of Ivy. She left the light on for her. Malena closed and padlocked the door.

Malena was nervous. She didn't know what else to do. She couldn't let Ivy tell Malik the truth about Ashley. She would have to keep Ivy in the storage room until she figured out what to do. Malena headed upstairs. She cut off the basement lights. As soon as she opened the basement door to go into the kitchen, she ran into Malik.

Malena: (*Startled.*) Malik?

Malik: What are you doing down there?

At the Hospital

Diane: What are the steps I need to take to get this done?

Dr. Baker: You will need a DNA test done. But before we jump to that, I think you need to talk to your sons first and let them know what you remember.

Diane: Yes, you are right. What about Kennedy and Jackson? I really don't know them and for me to pop out of nowhere with this will make me look suspicious.

Dr. Baker: (Grabbing her gently.) Let me talk to them. We go way back and are really close. I can make them understand. I can't promise, though, what kind of reaction I will get.

Diane hugged him.

Diane: Thank you, Joshua. I don't know what I would do without you.

The doctor kissed her on the forehead.

Dr. Baker: No problem. Now my shift is over, and I am ready to get out of here.

They both laughed.

Diane: I am sorry for keeping you here.

Dr. Baker: It's okay. I'm here for you. Now what I want you to do is go home and get some rest and talk to your sons tomorrow. I will let you know once I have spoken with Kennedy and Jackson.

Diane: Okay.

As soon as they got out the office, Dr. Baker was being paged to the nurse's station for an emergency. Dr. Baker and Diane rushed over to the station.

Dr. Baker: What's the emergency?

Nurse: Dr. Baker, I just wanted to catch you before you left. The ambulance was just dispatched out. Two men fell from the fourth floor of an apartment complex.

Diane: Oh my God.

Nurse: I didn't want you to make it all the way home then have to turn right around and come back.

Dr. Baker: Do they know how bad it is?

Nurse: No, the ambulance hasn't made it there yet.

Dr. Baker: Okay, thanks

Dr. Baker: (Turning to Diane.) The life of a doctor. Looks like I need to stay here after all.

Diane: Oh, I completely understand. I hope those boys are okay. Well, I will talk to you tomorrow.

Dr. Baker: Okay, drive safe.

The doctor gave her a kiss on the cheek and Diane left.

On the next episode, Malena asks for help.

Episode 3

Mystery and Mason lay unconscious on the concrete parking lot while Clay watched from his fourth-floor balcony. He could not believe what had just happened. He ran out the apartment and down the stairs. People had started gathering around the bodies.

Clay: (Yelling.) Someone call an ambulance!

One of the bystanders: I already have.

Clay ran to Mystery as he laid there unconscious. "Hold on, Mystery. The ambulance is coming." He began to cry. Clay looked up and saw Mason not far from Mystery lying unconscious as well. He ran over to him. "Mason, hold on, okay? The ambulance is on the way." Clay could hear to ambulance coming through the complex.

All of a sudden, two ambulances pulled up. The paramedics jumped out, two went to Mason and two to Mystery. They put oxygen masks on them both.

Lead paramedic: Can someone tell me what happened?

"Yes, I can," Clay said. "They were fighting and both fell from my apartment up there," pointing up to his apartment balcony.

Lead paramedic: What are their names?

Clay: (Pointing at Mystery.) His name is Mystery and the other guy is Mason.

Lead paramedic: Okay. We are going to take them to Emory. You can ride with one of them if you like.

Clay: Okay.

The paramedics loaded both Mason and Mystery into the ambulances. Clay got in with Mystery, and then they left headed to Emory Hospital.

MALIK'S HOUSE

Malena: (Grabbing her chest.) Malik, you scared me. What are you doing back here? You haven't too long left.

Malik: I left some papers that needed to be turned in today. What are you doing down there?

Malena: Oh, nothing, just had some boxes I needed to take down there.

Malik: You need help with something before I leave again.

Malena: Oh no, I'm finished now.

Malik: You sure?

Malena: Yes, baby.

Malik: Okay. Where is Ivy?

Malena: She . . . she went upstairs to use the bathroom.

Malik: Oh, okay. Well, I'm leaving then. Love you.

Malena: Love you too.

Malik gave her a kiss and left.

Malena watched Malik through the window to make sure he was gone. She then went to get the phone and made a call. She had to leave a message. "I need you to come by my house tomorrow as soon as possible. Malik will not be here. I need your help."

AT THE HOSPITAL

Dr. Baker, along with two other doctors, Dr. Walker and Dr. Spencer, was waiting at the nurse's station for the ambulances to come. About ten minutes later, the first ambulance pulled up with Mason. The paramedics jumped out and ran to the back. They got him out of the ambulance and rolled the stretcher quickly though the hospital doors. Dr. Baker and the other two doctors met them.

Dr. Baker: What do we have?

Paramedic: Patient's name is Mason. He fell from a fourth-floor apartment building and landed on his left side. He is having problems moving his left arm and leg.

Mason was conscious now and yelling out in pain. Dr. Baker gave him some morphine to help with the pain.

Dr. Baker: Mason, I am Dr. Baker. You're at Emory Hospital. The medicine I gave you will kick in shortly. We're going to take you down to get some X-rays so we know how to treat you. Okay, buddy.

Mason didn't say anything, just moaned in pain.

Dr. Baker: Dr. Walker, I will let you take this one, and I will wait on the other one.

Dr. Walker: Okay.

Dr. Walker left with Mason heading down to the X-ray department.

Dr. Spencer: The other ambulance is here.

The paramedics jumped out and rushed to the back. They got Mystery out and quickly rushed him into the hospital. Mystery was still unconscious.

Dr. Baker and Dr. Spencer both rushed to the paramedic. Dr. Baker didn't realize that it was Mystery.

Dr. Baker: What do we have?

Paramedic: Patient fell from the fourth floor of an apartment building. He hasn't regained consciousness the whole time. Patient landed on his back and was bleeding out the mouth.

Dr. Spencer: Sounds like internal bleeding.

Dr. Baker: I agree. Let's get a breathing tube in him and down to X-ray immediately. We have to find out where this internal bleeding is coming from. What's his name?

Paramedic: Mystery.

Dr. Baker paused. He slowly looked down at Mystery closely.

Dr. Baker: Oh my God. I didn't . . .

Clay: Dad?

Dr. Baker looked up and saw Clay standing there crying.

On the next episode, Kennedy and his wife gets an unexpected visitor.

Episode 4

Malena didn't go to bed at all last night. She had fallen asleep on the sofa. All of a sudden, there was a knock on the door. Malena jumped up quick, frightened. She then realized that she had made a call last night and was expecting someone. She went to answer the door. When she opened the door, it was Armon. Malena just broke down crying, putting her hands over her face. Armon embraced her to comfort her.

Armon: Hey, hey, what's wrong? Why are you so upset?

Malena (crying): I don't know what to do.

Armon: I'm here now, little sis. Tell me what's wrong.

Malena (crying hysterically): Armon, I didn't mean to do it. I swear. I tried to talk to her.

Armon: Malena, you have to calm down. Look at me.

Malena looked at Armon.

Armon: You know I got your back no matter what. Now tell me what's going on.

Malena: (Wiping her eyes.) I've done something terrible.

Armon: I'm sure it's not that bad.

Malena: Follow me.

Armon followed her through the kitchen down to the basement.

Armon: It's dusty down here. You guys don't come down here often, do you?

Malena didn't respond. She went over to the storage room and unlocked the door. She opened the door and stepped back so Armon could look inside. Armon was shocked by what he was seeing. He saw Ivy tied up to a chair with her head hanging down. He turned and faced Malena.

Armon: What have you done?

ALEXANDRIA'S PLACE

Alexandria woke up sick this morning. She had been feeling bad the last few days. She couldn't keep anything down, and it seems everything she ate made her sick. She decided to get up and cook breakfast still. She had to feed her son.

While Alexandria was cooking, her cell phone rang. She saw it was Brazil. She and Brazil had been spending a lot of time together. He was even spending nights over and Alexandria was loving every bit of it. They couldn't keep their hands off each other. Jase was getting used to seeing Brazil but as a child still had reservations. Alexandria answered the phone.

Alexandria: Hello?

Brazil: Hey, beautiful.

Alexandria: If you could see me this morning, you wouldn't be saying that.

Brazil: (Laughing.) Why you say that?

Alexandria: I'm not feeling well.

Brazil: Again? You need to go to the doctor seriously.

Alexandria: I know. I'm going to give it another day and see if it will pass. If not then I will make an appointment. What are you doing?

Brazil: Just here working, looking over some papers. It looks like I will be going to North Carolina for a few days. I need to follow up on a lead for this case I have.

Alexandria: Oh, okay, when are you leaving?

Brazil: In the morning.

Alexandria: So soon? Are you coming back over tonight?

Brazil: Wouldn't be any place else.

They both laughed.

Brazil: As soon as I finish up here, I will be over. Talk to you soon.

Alexandria: Okay, have a good day. Bye.

They both hung up.

Alexandria: (Yelling.) Jase it's time to eat.

Jase ran from the back room. Alexandria set their plates on the table and they began to eat.

AT THE HOSPITAL

Dr. Baker: Clay?

Dr. Baker could hardly recognize his own son. Clay's face was swollen and one of his eyes was completely swollen shut. He was in a trance looking at his son's face.

Dr. Spencer: Doctor? Doctor?

Dr. Baker snapped out of his trance. "Yes, Dr. Spencer, get this patient to X-ray now. We need to see where this internal bleeding is coming from and stop it.

Dr. Spencer: Okay.

Dr. Spencer rushed Mystery to X-ray. Dr. Baker turned back to look at Clay.

Clay: (Crying.) This is all my fault, Dad.

Dr. Baker didn't say a word. He just went to his son and hugged him.

Dr. Baker: Nurse? (Calling for one of the nurses behind the nurse's station.)

Nurse: Yes, Doctor.

Dr. Baker: I need you to tend to my son's face and clean him up.

Nurse: Okay.

Clay: Dad, I'm okay. I need to go make sure Mystery is okay.

Dr. Baker: Have you looked in a mirror? You are going to stay here and let the nurse bandage and clean your face up. Afterward, you wait in my office. I'm going to make sure Mystery is okay. I need to go to him now though.

Dr. Baker left and the nurse took Clay to a room.

BRAZIL'S HOUSE

Brazil has finished up his work and was about to walk out the door when his cell phone rang.

Brazil: Hello?

Kathy: May I speak with Brazil please.
Brazil: This is Brazil. How can I help you?

Kathy: My name is Kathy. I was given your name and number as an emergency contact by Ivy.

Brazil stopped in his tracks.

Brazil: Okay, is something wrong?

Kathy: Well, I don't know. She left Ivan over my house yesterday evening to play with my son, and she never came back.

Brazil: (Confused.) What do you mean she never came back?

Kathy: Ivan spent the night over my house last night. Ivy haven't called or anything. I'm starting to worry.

Brazil: That doesn't sound like Ivy. Okay, text me your address, and I will come get Ivan. I will try to get in touch Ivy.

Kathy: Okay.

They both hung up. Brazil called Ivy's phone and got her voice mail so he left a message.

Brazil: Ivy, where are you? Kathy just called me and said you left our son with her overnight and have not called or anything. This is not like you. What is going on? Call me as soon as you get this. I am going to go pick up Ivan.

Brazil hung up and headed to go pick up Ivan.

KENNEDY'S HOUSE

Kennedy and his wife Rebecca were watching television when their doorbell rang.

Rebecca: I'll get it. Are you expecting anybody?

Kennedy: No.

Rebecca went to answer the door. When she opened the door, she was surprised.

Rebecca: Caleb?

Caleb: Hey, Mom.

On the next episode, Malena tells Armon the truth about Ashley.

Episode 5

Armon: Malena, what have you done? Is she dead?

Malena: No.

Armon: Are you sure?

Armon grabbed Ivy's wrist to see if he could feel a pulse. He did.

Armon: Okay, I feel it. What happened?

Malena: She was going to tell Malik my secret, and I couldn't let her do that. I can't lose my husband, Armon. I can't.

Armon: You won't. Now tell me. What is this secret she has on you to make you do this?

Malena: I can't say.

Armon: (Grabbing his sister's hand.) Do you trust me?

Malena: Of course I do. I wouldn't have asked for your help if I didn't.

Armon: Okay then, tell me. You are my sister, and I love you. There isn't anything you could have done to make me turn my back on you. We always had each other's backs growing up, didn't we?

Malena: Yeah.

Armon: Okay then, what is it? I need to know exactly what I'm dealing with if I'm going to help you.

Malena: (Crying.) She overheard me talking on the phone about Ashley.

Armon: What about Ashley?

Armon already knew what Malena was about to say because he has been blackmailing Max with the same information.

Malena: She is not Malik's child.

KENNEDY'S HOUSE

Rebecca: Caleb, my baby.

Rebecca was overjoyed to see her son. He had been away in prison for five years for rape. While he was locked up all this time, he didn't allow his mother or father to come see him. Although Kennedy and Rebecca wanted to, Caleb didn't want it. He saw during the court procedures how big of a toll, what he did, was putting on his family. He was not going to have it continue for five more years after he left.

Rebecca just hugged him tight. She placed her hands on his face.

Rebecca: Your father is going to be so happy to see you. Come on.

They walked in the living room.

Rebecca: Kennedy, look who's here.

Kennedy turned around and saw his son standing there. He stood up.

Caleb: Dad.

Kennedy: Caleb, my son.

Kennedy grabbed his son and hugged him tight. Rebecca could only cry and smile with happiness.

KATHY'S HOUSE

Brazil had made it to Kathy's house. He knocked on the door and a lady came to answer.

Kathy: Yes?

Brazil: My name is Brazil, Ivan's dad. Are you Kathy?

Kathy: Oh yes, come in. Have you heard from Ivy?

Brazil: Unfortunately, no. I left her a voice mail to call me as soon as possible.

Kathy: I hope everything is okay with her. One second, I will go get Ivan.

Kathy went to her son's bedroom where the boys were playing the video game.

Kathy: Ivan, your dad is here to get you. Say goodbye, Sam.

Sam: Bye, Ivan.

Ivan: Bye.

Kathy and Ivan walked back to Brazil.

Ivan: Dad!

Ivan was always happy to see and be with his dad.

Brazil: All ready to go, bud?

Ivan: Yep. Where is Mom?

Brazil: We're about to go find her now. Thanks, Kathy, for watching him. I'm sorry if it was any inconvenience.

Kathy: Oh no, it wasn't at all. Ivan is welcome over anytime. Please call me and let me know Ivy is okay when you find her.

Brazil: I will.

Brazil and Ivan left. When they got in the car, Brazil tried to call Ivy again. It went straight to her voice mail. He started to get worry now because it had been twenty-four hours.

Ivan: Dad, is everything okay with Mom?

Brazil: I sure hope so, son. Let's go visit someone that may know.

Brazil pulled off and left.

MALIK'S HOUSE

Armon: What do you mean she's not Malik?

Malena: Malik is not her father.

Armon had to play along. He didn't want her to know that he already knew.

Armon: (Speaking slowly.) Oh, okay.

He hugged her.

Armon: It's going to be okay, sis. I'm going to help you take care of everything. First thing first, let's go back upstairs before the girls get up and catch us down here.

Malena closed the storage room door and locked it. They went back upstairs to the living room.

Armon: Is that her car out there?

Malena: (Nervous.) Yes. What are we going to do with it?

Armon: You let me worry about that. Where are the keys?

Malena: I think she left them in the car.

Armon: Okay, perfect. You go upstairs and get yourself together. Come back down and cook breakfast like nothing has happen. I will be back as soon as I can. If Malik asks about her, just say she left late last night.

Malena: Okay.

Malena hugged him and said, "I love you. Be careful."

Armon: Everything is going to be okay.

Armon went outside to check the car for the keys. Keys were in the ignition. He got in and left. Malena went upstairs to get herself together.

On the next episode, Dr. Baker gives Clay the news about Mason and Mystery.

Episode 6

Max and Adriana were lying in the bed talking when Adriana's cell phone rang. She recognize that it was Alexandria calling.

Adriana: Hold on, Max. It's Alexandria. Hello?

Jase: Hey, Aunt Adriana.

Adriana: Jase? Hey, baby, are you okay?

Jase: It's Mom.

Adriana sat up in the bed.

Adriana: What about your mom?

Jase: She's sick. She keeps throwing up and won't get out the bed.

Adriana: Let me talk to her.

Jase: She doesn't know I called you.

Adriana: Okay, baby, we'll be over in a little bit okay.

Jase: Okay.

They both hung up.

Max: Is everything okay?

Adriana: Jase said Alexandria is sick. We need to go over there and check on her.

Max: Of course. It must have Jase nervous for him to call.

They both got up to get dressed.

AT THE HOSPITAL

Clay was in his dad's office waiting. The nurse had cleaned and bandaged the cuts on his face. His jaw and one of his eyes were swollen. As he sat there, the only thing he could think about was Mystery. As soon as he stood up to walk out, his dad walked in.

Clay: Dad.

Dr. Baker didn't say anything. He just stared at his son for a second.

Clay: Dad, how are they?

Dr. Baker: Clay it's not good for either one of them. Mason has a broken leg, arm, and hip, all on his left side. He is resting now in the recovery room and will wake up as the medicine begins to wear off.

Clay: What about Mystery?

Dr. Baker: We had to do emergency surgery on Mystery because he had internal bleeding we needed to stop. By him landing on his back, the blunt force punctured both of his kidneys.

Clay: Oh my God.

Dr. Baker: We stopped the bleeding and repaired his kidneys as best we can. We now have to wait and keep check to make sure they continue to function as usual. If not then he will need a kidney transplant.

Clay: Can I see him?

Dr. Baker: No, Clay, you can't. What you can do is tell me what the hell happen and now.

Clay: Dad.

Dr. Baker: (Raising his voice.) Now, Clay!

ALEXANDRIA'S PLACE

Alexandria was in the bedroom lying down. Jase was in the living room watching TV when there was a knock at the door. Jase ran to the bedroom.

Jase: Mom, someone is at the door.

Alexandria just moaned.

There was another knock at the door. Jase ran to the door.

Jase: Who is it?

Max: Jase, it's your Uncle Max and Aunt Adriana.

Adriana: Open the door, baby.

Jase opened the door for them to come in.

MYSTERY

Adriana: Where's your mom?

Jase: She's in the bed.

Max and Adriana went to the bedroom. Alexandria was in the bed under the covers.

Adriana: Alexandria? Alexandria, honey, what's wrong?

Alexandria just moaned then said, "Hey, what you guys doing here?"

Adriana looked at Jase. She knew not to say anything about him calling them.

Adriana: We just decided to come over and check on you. Good thing we did.

Adriana felt Alexandria's head.

Adriana: Oh my God, girl, you are burning up and these sheets are soaked and wet. Okay, come on, we're going to the hospital.

Alexandria: I'm okay. I took something earlier.

Adriana: Evidently, it's not working. Let's go. Max, help me get her up.

Max helped Adriana to get Alexandria to her feet. Alexandria would have fallen to the floor if Max hadn't caught her. She was very weak. Max picked her up in his arms and headed for the door. As soon as they opened the door to walk out, they ran into Armon.

Armon: What's going on here?

On the next episode, Clay confesses everything to his father.

Episode 7

Dr. Baker didn't know what to think looking at his son with his swollen face.

Dr. Baker: What happened?

Clay: All this is my fault.

Dr. Baker: I sure hope not. Both of those guys are not out of the woods, Clay. They have a long recovery ahead of them. You do know the police, more than likely your brother, will be here to question them, don't you?

Clay: No, why?

Dr. Baker: Clay, they're going to want to know what happened and to find out who was at fault here. The dispatch came in that two guys were fighting at an apartment complex and fell from the fourth floor. This doesn't look good for either one of them. Now you need to tell me what happed.

Clay: I don't know where to start.

Dr. Baker: You can start by telling me why they were fighting in the first place.

Clay dropped his head.

Clay: They were fighting over me.

Dr. Baker: What do you mean they were fighting over you?

Clay could not hold it in any longer. He had to tell his dad the truth so he just blurted it out.

Clay: Dad, Mystery and I are in love with each other and have been for a very long time.

Clay and his dad just stared at each other. Clay didn't know what kind of response he was going to get from him. He just knew he couldn't keep it from his dad any longer.

Clay: Dad, did you hear what I said?

Dr. Baker took a deep breath. He put his hand on his son's shoulder and said, "It's okay, son. I already knew that."

ALEXANDRIA'S PLACE

Armon: What's going here? What's wrong with Alexandria?

Adriana: Move out of our way, Armon. We don't have time to talk to you right now. We are going to the hospital.

Armon: I'm her husband. I have a right to know what's wrong with my wife.

Adriana: Really, Armon? You want to play the husband card again because it's getting old quick. Now move.

Adriana pushed passed him with Max right behind her carrying Alexandria in his arms. Jase didn't say anything to his father.

Armon: Well, I'm following you to the hospital.

Adriana: Whatever.

They all left for Emory Hospital.

Malik's House

Malik was on his way to the hospital from work. Malena had taken the girls to the mall. She needed to get out of the house and clear her head a little. There was no one in the house but Ivy. Ivy began to wake up. She opened her eyes slowly. She could hardly see. Everything was a blur. All of a sudden, she felt pain coming from the back of her head. She moaned out. She went to reach for her head but realized she couldn't. She didn't know what was going on. Vision still blurry, Ivy closed her eyes and counted to five. She then reopened them. Her vision was becoming clearer. She looked around to see where she was but couldn't figure out where. Her vision was becoming even clearer now and getting back to its normal state. Ivy then notice she was in some kind of storage room. She went to stand up but noticed she couldn't. Ivy looked down at her hands and saw that she was duct-taped to the chair. She immediately realized that her mouth was duct-taped as well. She tried to free herself but couldn't. The tape had her tied down tight. Ivy yelled out but the duct-tape smothered her voice. She began to wonder who could have put her in here like this and left her. She didn't know where she was. She started to look around for anything that could tell her where she may be. She didn't see anything. All she saw were old clothes, boxes, and two bicycles. Ivy yelled out again but no sound could come out.

Ivy continued to struggle trying to get herself free. The tape started to loosen up around one of her ankles, and she felt it. Ivy looked around again. She noticed one of the boxes next to her had some writing on it. She could only make out the word "things" but could not make out the first word because it was being covered by a shirt sleeve that was lying on top of it.

Ivy started to become tired with all the struggling trying to get loose. She rested herself for a minute then started back. She continued to work to get her ankle free since it was the most loose. She put all her force and energy in her leg. She worked and wiggled her leg and stretched the tape until it broke from around her ankle. Ivy was relieved and completely exhausted.

She reached her leg over and kicked the box knocking the shirt off, in doing that revealing the words, "Malik's Things." Ivy, shocked, realized then she was in her brother's basement but how. She started to think, and then she remembered. "It was Malena," she said to herself.

AT THE HOSPITAL

Max and Adriana made it to the hospital with Alexandria. Armon was right there to as he had followed them there. Alexandria was still weak, coughing, and sweating heavily. Max had to carry her inside. Adriana went to sign her in while the rest of them took seats in the waiting room.

Armon: Jase, come seat next to me, son.

Jase didn't say anything. He wouldn't even look at his dad.

Armon: Jase?

Jase continued to ignore him. Max looked at Jase, then at Armon. Armon had this angry look on his face. Then he shook he head and said, "Max, how is Ashley?"

Max, whispering nervously, said, "What are you doing? Don't you see Adriana right there?"

Even though Adriana didn't hear him because she was busy getting Alexandria signed it, it still made Max nervous.

Armon: Yes, I see her. You think I care about that. It seems you haven't done what I told you.

Max: I haven't had the time.

Armon: You better make time and fast because I'm not going to be dealing with this rejection for something you did. This is your last and final warning.

Max looked at Jase.

Max. Jase, are you okay?

Jase: Yes, I just want Mom to feel better.

Max: Will you do me a favor and go sit by your dad? We don't want you to catch whatever it is your mom has.

Jase: But you are sitting next to her, will you catch it?

Max: Nooooo, because I am strong. So do this for me and go sit by him, okay?

Jase: (Slowly.) Okay.

Jase slowly walked over to Armon with his head down and sat next to him.

Armon: Hey, li'l man.

Jase: Hey.

Adriana walked up. She saw that Jase was sitting next to Armon and started to say something, but Max cut her off.

Max: Babe, I told Jase to go over there and sit because I didn't want him to catch whatever it is Alexandria has.

Adriana: Oh, okay.

She looked at Armon and rolled her eyes then took a seat.

Adriana: Her doctor is actually here in the hospital. The nurse said he should be down in a few.

Alexandria had her head laid over on Max's shoulder. She was terribly sick and had everyone worried even Armon.

On the next episode, Armon threatens Max.

Episode 8

Kennedy, Rebecca, and Caleb were all sitting at the kitchen table. Even though Kennedy and Rebecca weren't expecting to see their son for another month, they were both overjoyed he was home.

Kennedy: We are so happy to have you home, son. Why didn't you call us? We would have come to pick you up.

Caleb: I know. I just wanted to surprise you both.

Rebecca: Well, you did that.

Rebecca got up and kissed her son on his head. "Now I know you have to be hungry. What do you want to eat? Want me to fix your favorite?"

Caleb: Mom, you know I can never resist your lasagna.

They all laughed, and Rebecca started to prepare the lasagna.

Caleb: How is Sarah?

Kennedy: Your sister is doing really well for herself. She lives and works for this law firm in Alpharetta. She will be here tomorrow. She always comes by on the weekends to visit.

Caleb: I can't wait to see her. What about Ana? Have you heard from her?

When Caleb asked that, everything came to a halt. Complete silence filled the room. Rebecca stopped what she was doing and looked over at Kennedy. Caleb looked at both his parents.

Caleb: Well, Dad? Mom? Have you heard from her?

AT THE HOSPITAL

Adrianna: (Getting frustrated.) What is taking so long?

As soon as she said that, Dr. Walker walked into the waiting room. He knew Alexandria well as he was her primary doctor. They all stood up.

Adriana: Are you Dr. Walker?

Dr. Walker: Yes, I am. I'm Alexandria's doctor.

Adriana: She is very sick, Doctor. She can't walk. She will not eat anything. Anything she tries to eat, she brings back up.

Dr. Walker kneeled down in front of Alexandria.

Dr. Walker: Alexandria, can you hear me?

Alexandria: (Coughing.) Yes.

Dr. Walker: I am going to take your temperature, okay?

Dr. Walker put a thermometer in her mouth. When he checked the results, he saw her temperature was 104.

Dr. Walker: Her temperature is too high. I'm going to have her admitted so we can get this temperature down. That way I can run some more tests as well. I will have the nurse come get her and take her to a room. I have some papers that need filling out and signing. Who is her next of kin?

Adriana: I am. I'm her sister.

Before the doctor could respond, Armon blurted out, "I am. I am her husband."

Adriana: (With an attitude.) Are you serious right now. Doctor, he is right. He is the husband. He is the same husband that put her in the hospital after beating her.

Armon was livid.

Armon: (Raising his voice.) Go to hell, Adriana!

Raising her voice right back, Adriana said, "No, you go to hell. You are a pathetic excuse for a husband."

Armon: And you think you have the perfect husband?

Adriana: I know I do.

Armon was fixing to tell her the truth about Max, but Dr. Walker interrupted.

Dr. Walker: Okay, everyone needs to calm down. This is a hospital.

Dr. Walker: (Addressing Adriana.) I'm sorry, miss, but since he is the husband, he is considered the next of kin.

Armon: You know what, Doctor? She can do it.

Dr. Walker: Are you sure?

Armon: Yes.

Armon only let this go because he needed a few moments with Max. The nurse came with a wheelchair to get Alexandria. Max helped her get in the chair then she and the nurse left.

Dr. Walker: I will let you all know once we get her settled in a room.

Turning to Adriana, the doctor said, "Follow me," then they went to his office.

Armon walked over to Max.

Armon: You need to learn to keep your bitch on a tighter leash.

Max got in Armon's face. "Don't you ever talk about my wife like that."

Armon: Or what? What are you going to do, baby daddy?

Max just stared at him with hate in his eyes.

Armon: Nothing, just like I thought. Now I advise you to go over there and talk to my son and make things right with us.

Max didn't move or say a word. He wanted to hit Armon so bad he could taste it.

Armon: I don't like repeating myself or maybe I should just talk to the wifey when she comes back since she thinks you're Mr. Perfect.

Max walked past Armon and bumped him. He went over to Jase to talk to him. A few minutes later, Adriana came back, and they all waited for the doctor to return with the test results.

MALIK'S HOUSE

Ivy was furious with Malena for hitting her over the head and locking her in the basement. Ivy knew she couldn't do anything because she was taped to the chair. She continued to struggle and wrestle with the tape to try and get free but couldn't. All of a sudden, she heard footsteps coming from upstairs. She tried to scream out but couldn't.

Malena and the girls had made it back from the mall. Malena knew she needed to go check on Ivy.

Malena: Girls, go wash up and get ready for bed. I will be up there in a minute. Melanie, don't be on that cell phone when I come up there.

Melanie: Mom, come on now.

Malena: You hear me, don't you? It's late. You can talk to your little boyfriend tomorrow.

They headed upstairs. Malena waited for a few minutes then headed to the basement. Ivy could hear someone coming. She was hoping it was Malik. Malena unlock the door and opened it. She saw that Ivy was awake now. Ivy had this evil look in her eyes. Malena spoke nervously, "Ivy I'm so sorry for this. I just panic."

Malena could see that Ivy was trying to say something but couldn't.

Malena: I'm going to take the tape off your mouth but you can't yell out.

Ivy didn't motion or say anything. Malena peeled the tape off of her mouth. Ivy looked at her with hatred in her eyes and said, "Cut me loose, now."

On the next episode, Armon gets unexpected news.

Episode 9

Clay: Dad, how could you have known about me and Mystery?

Dr. Baker: Son, I may be older, but I'm not dumb. I'm your father. I've known for a while now. The way you two acted around each other and how you would just light up when Mystery used to come over to visit Malik. Your mother knew about the two of you way before I did.

Clay: What do you mean?

Dr. Baker: Before you came out to us that you were gay, your mom had already mentioned it to me.

Clay: She never said anything to me or treated me differently.

Dr. Baker: Of course she wouldn't treat you differently. She was your mother and loved you with all her heart. She told me that you would tell us when you were ready, so we waited.

Clay smiled to himself.

Clay: I miss her so much, Dad.

Dr. Baker hugged his son and said, "Me too, son. Me too."

There was a knock at the door.

Dr. Baker: Come in.

Malik walked in. He saw Clay standing there with his face all swollen and bandage up. Clay could tell by the look on Malik's face that he was angry about it.

Dr. Baker: Malik, come on in, son.

Malik: Hey, Dad. Clay, what happened to your face?

Before he could speak, Malik interrupted. "Wait. Mason did this, didn't he?"

"Yes," Clay said.

Dr. Baker: Wait a second, Clay. You didn't tell me this. Did Mason beat you like this?

Clay: Dad, I didn't want you to worry. I was handling it.

Dr. Baker: Evidently not if you are looking like this. We are definitely going to have a talk about this.

Malik: Well, Dad, I'm here on official police business this time. I've come to get statements from the two guys that fell from the balcony if they can talk.

Dr. Baker: Son, those two guys were Mason and Mystery.

Malik: What!

KENNEDY'S HOUSE

Caleb: Mom, Dad? Have you heard from Ana?

Kennedy: No, son, we haven't.

Caleb: (Getting upset.) What do you mean, you haven't. You promised me when I went away you would talk to her and stay in contact with her.

Rebecca: Caleb, we tried. She didn't want us to contact her or anything. The last time we spoke to her was at your sentencing. She told us that she wanted nothing to do with you and that she was moving away. What were we supposed to do?

Caleb stood up. "I have to try and find her."

Kennedy raised his voice, "Caleb sit down!"

MALIK'S HOUSE

Ivy: Cut me loose, now.

Malena: Ivy, I can't do that.

Ivy: What do you mean? What do you plan on doing, Malena? You can't keep me down here forever.

Malena: I know that. I just need to keep you here until I figure out what I'm going to do.

Ivy: Malena, you can't do this. This is kidnapping. You can go to jail for this.

Malena: You gave me no choice. You were going to tell Malik everything. You weren't supposed to find out that Ashley wasn't his child. I had everything under control. Now you have messed everything up.

Ivy: He has every right to know the truth. How long you think you could have kept this a secret?

Malena: As long as I needed to. Malik is my husband, and I love him.

Malena started to cry. "I made a terrible mistake and he will never forgive me for it."

Ivy: How do you know that? Malik loves you. It's nothing that you two can't work out.

Ivy was just saying this to get Malena to let her guard down. She needed to do and say whatever she could to get Malena to free her.

Malena: (Wiping her eyes.) You think so?

Ivy: Of course I do. I can be there with you when you tell him if you like. You're my sister-in-law no matter what and I love you too.

Ivy could tell she was getting to Malena. Malena was thinking. "I don't know. I will be taking a huge risk."

Melanie called out from the kitchen, "Mom?"

Both Malena and Ivy heard her. Ivy yelled out, "MELANIE, DOWN HERE!"

Malena forced the tape back on Ivy's mouth. She ran out the storage room, slamming it shut, forgetting to lock it back. By the time she made it to the stairs, Melanie was coming down the stairs.

At the Hospital

Adriana, Max, and Armon were still waiting for the doctor to return. It had been over an hour. Jase had fallen asleep. Everyone was getting tired. Max had his head laid back against the wall. Adriana had her head laid on Max's shoulder. Armon was sitting there staring at them both. Adriana lifted her hear and saw him staring at them.

Adriana: What are you staring at?

Armon: You.

Adriana: I don't even know why you're still here. No one wants you here.

Armon: Which is exactly the reason why I'm staying.

Max: Let it go, babe.

A few minutes later, the doctor came in. They all stood up.

Adriana: How is she, Doctor?

Dr. Walker: Alexandria has a bad case of the flu. It's good you got her here when you did. This could have easily turned into pneumonia. She was also dehydrated. I have given her medication to help get her temperature down. I have also given her fluids to rehydrate her.

Max: Is she going to be okay?

Dr. Walker: Yes, she is going to be fine. The medication will help get her temperature back to normal. However, I am going to keep her here for a few days so I can keep monitoring them both.

Adriana: Wait a minute. Monitor them both?

Dr. Walker: (Smiling.) Yes, Alexandria is pregnant.

Armon: What?

Dr. Walker: (Addressing Armon.) Congratulations. You're going to be a father.

On the next episode, Dr. Baker warns Mason.

Episode 10

Malik was shocked. "Did you say Mason and Mystery were the two guys that fell?"

Dr. Baker: I'm afraid so, son.

Malik: Wow. Are they going to be okay?

Dr. Baker: Well, Mystery is sedated right now. I have him resting. I'm waiting to see if his kidneys are going to continue to function normally so you will not be able to talk to him right now. Mason has a broken leg, arm, and hip. He is probably awake by now.

Malik: Okay, well, I need to talk to him.

Dr. Baker: Let me go check on him first and make sure he is up. Wait for me here.

The doctor left to go check on Mason. Malik looked at Clay.

Malik: Tell me what happened.

Meanwhile, the doctor headed to Mason's room. When he got to his room, he just watched him from the door. Mason turned his head and saw the doctor standing there.

Mason: Doctor, please can you give me something? I am in so much pain.

Dr. Baker just stood there staring at Mason.

Mason: Doc?

Dr. Baker snapped out of his trance.

Dr. Baker: Huh . . . oh no, you can't have anything else right now. It's not time.

Dr. Baker went on into the room and closed the door behind.

Dr. Baker: I have something else I need to talk to you about though.

Mason: (Grunting.) About what?

Dr. Baker: You know I remember you. When you were younger, you used to come to my house and hang out with my son Malik, you and Mystery both.

Mason: Yea, so.

Dr. Baker: I am assuming by what has taken place you all are not close anymore.

Mason: No, we're not.

Dr. Baker: But you are close with my other son Clay, aren't you? Really close.

Mason: What are you getting at?

Dr. Baker: Clay told me everything that happened tonight. He is giving his statement to the police as we speak. The police will be in to speak with you shortly, but I wanted to talk to you first.

Mason: About what?

Dr. Baker leaned over and got in Mason's face.

Dr. Baker: I am a doctor, but I am a father first. If you ever put your hands on my son again, a fall from a fourth-floor balcony will be the least of your worries. Don't let this clean-cut professional doctor fool you because when it comes to someone hurting my children, I'm a totally different person. Do I make myself clear?

Mason didn't say anything, but he knew that the doctor meant business by what he was saying.

Dr. Baker: Now I am going to give your charts and paperwork to Dr. Spencer. He will be your main doctor going forward. I think that's best for the both of us.

Dr. Baker left and Mason just laid there in pain staring at the ceiling.

KENNEDY'S HOUSE

Kennedy: Listen, son, do you want to go back to jail?

Caleb: Of course not.

Kennedy: Then you need to stay away from her. You hear me? She made it perfectly clear to us that she didn't want you contacting her for any reason from prison or out of prison. That's why she changed her number and moved away. We had no way of tracking her down.

Caleb: I can't believe she would do that.

Kennedy: Son you raped her. What did you expect? Honestly.

Caleb: Dad, I was drunk. I wasn't trying to hurt her. Things just go out of control so fast. She was in fact my girlfriend no less.

Kennedy: Do you think that gave you the right to force yourself on her? Girlfriend or not, when a woman says no, she means no.

Rebecca: Okay, let us all take a breather. Caleb, we just got you back home. We don't want you doing anything that may put you back in that godforsaken place. Your dad and I love you and want what is best and right now trying to find Ana is not the best thing you can do. You have to move on, baby.

Caleb: I just wanted to tell her face-to-face how sorry I was and that I regretted what I did.

Rebecca: We know how sorry you are, but it is over with now and you have done your time for it. It's time for you to move on and make a new life for yourself.

Caleb: Okay, I guess you are right.

Kennedy: She is, son. We wouldn't lie to you about this.

Caleb: I know. I am going to go upstairs and take a shower.

Caleb left the kitchen. Kennedy put his arm around his wife for comfort.

At the Hospital

Malik: This fight between Mason and Mystery happened at your apartment?

Clay: Yes.

Malik: I'm going to have to take your statement.

Clay: I understand.

Malik got out the pad and pencil he had brought with him.

Malik: Okay, tell me what happened?

Clay: I told Mason today that I didn't want to be in a relationship with him anymore and that me and Mystery was getting back together.

Malik: Was Mystery aware that you were going to tell Mason?

Clay: Yes, he just didn't know it was going to be today. Mystery told me the only way we could be together was for me to tell Mason and make him understand that it was really over. Needless to say, he got angry and did this to me. (Pointing at his face.)

Malik: Go on.

Clay: He knocked me unconscious by kicking me in the face. When I came to, he was in the bathroom. That gave me the opportunity to sneak out the house. I somehow found myself at Mystery's front door. I must have blackout because everything from then on is a blur. I remember waking up on his sofa with a splitting headache. He had left me a note on the table.

Malik: What did the note say?

Clay: That he was sorry, but he couldn't let this go and that it ends tonight. I knew right then where he was headed. By the time I got to my apartment and got inside, it was too late. They both had gone over the balcony.

Clay started to choke up. "This is all my fault."

Malik rested his hand on Clay's shoulder. "None of this is your fault."

Dr. Baker came back in the office. You could tell he was angry.

Malik: Dad, are you okay?

Dr. Baker: Yea, I'm fine.

Clay: Are you sure?

Dr. Baker: (Taking a deep breath.) Yes, I am fine.

Malik: Okay well, I'm done questioning Clay. Is it okay to question Mason?

Dr. Baker: Yeah, go ahead, he's awake and lucid. He's in room 330.

Malik: Okay, once I finish with him, I'm going to head back to the station. I will talk to you both later.

Both Clay and Dr. Baker said okay and Malik left to go question Mason.

Clay: Dad, I know he is not awake, but I need to see Mystery.

Dr. Baker: Okay, go ahead. Just don't stay long. He's in room 348.

Clay: Thanks, Dad.

Clay left. The doctor sat down at his desk to collect his thoughts. About ten minutes later, there was a knock at his door.

Dr. Baker: Come in.

Brazil walked through the door with Ivan in his arms asleep. The doctor stood up slowly. It was like watching Mystery walk through his door.

Brazil: Hey, Dr. Baker. I'm Brazil, Ivy's ex-husband.

MALIK'S HOUSE

As Malena rushed to the staircase, Melanie was already coming down them.

Malena: (Nervously.) Melanie, what are you doing?

Melanie: You call me down here. Are you okay?

Malena: Yes, yes. Just saw a rat. That's all.

Melanie getting scared and looking around said, "Where? Where?"

Malena: Over there by the storage room. Let's go back upstairs.

Melanie: Sounds good to me. I hate rats.

They both headed back upstairs and into the kitchen.

Malena: Melanie, I don't want you girls going down there okay. It dirty and dusty down there and there aren't no telling what other kind of rodents are down there.

Melanie: You most definitely don't have to worry about me going down there at all. You might want to tell Ashley, though. I know she plays down there sometimes.

Malena: (Surprised.) Oh, she does?

Melanie: Yep.

Malena: Well let me go talk to her right now then.

They both headed upstairs.

At the Hospital

Armon, Adriana, and Max were all surprised by the news the doctor had given them.

Armon: Excuse me? What did you say?

Dr. Walker: You are going to be a father, congratulations.

Armon: (Confused.) That's not possible. Alexandria can't have any more children.

Dr. Walker: I can assure you, sir, it is possible. I did three separate test, and they all confirmed that Alexandria is pregnant.

Adrian: Doctor, how far along is she?

Dr. Walker: Almost two months.

Armon: (Furious.) Two months? How could she?

Adriana: Armon, please.

Armon looked at her with hate in his eyes.

Adriana: Doctor, that is great news.

Armon, angry, stormed out of the waiting room.

Dr. Walker: Is he going to be okay?

Adriana: He will be fine. He just upset because he knows that he is not the father.

Dr. Walker: Oh, I'm terribly sorry about that. I didn't know.

Adriana: I'm not sorry.

Max: Baby.

Adriana: What? I'm not. For what he put my sister through, I am not going to sugarcoat anything for that man. Doctor, when can we see her?

Dr. Walker: I can take you right now. I have already given her the news about the baby too.

Max picked up Jase because he was still asleep, then he and Adriana followed the doctor to Alexandria's room.

On the next episode, Ivy comes up with a plan.

Episode 11

Mason was lying in bed, asleep. It will take a lot of physical therapy after suffering from a broken leg, arm, and hip. His arm was in a cast. His leg was elevated in a cast as well. The doctors had him strapped to the bed to keep him from moving due to the broken hip.

Malik walked into the room without knocking and closed the door. The sound of the door closing woke Mason up.

Malik: Well, well, well.

Mason: What do you want?

Malik: I'm here on official police business to take your statement on what happened.

Mason: Get out. I don't have anything to say to you.

Malik: Are you refusing to give me your statement?

Mason: I'm refusing to talk to you.

Malik: You know you can go to jail if Clay presses charges.

Mason: And if he do I'll—

Malik leaned over in Mason's face and said, "If he do you'll what?" Malik punched Mason on his broken hip. Mason yelled out in pain. Malik put his hands over Mason's mouth to keep him from yelling out again. He punched him again on his broken hip. Mason yelled out again but no sound could escape. Mason was in so much pain. "Look at you. I don't think you are in any position to make threats." Malik removed his hand from Mason's mouth shoving his face. Mason was breathing hard. The pain was excruciating.

Malik: It's okay. You don't have to give me your statement today. I will wait until you're able to walk that way I can take your ass to the station.

Mason was grunting.

Malik: One last thing, stay away from Clay. I will be making sure he takes a restraining order out on you for this.

Malik left the room. Mason laid there in pain grunting and moaning.

MALIK'S HOUSE

Ivy continued to struggle to get free. She was wearing herself out. She hadn't eaten nor drank anything for the last twenty-four hours. Even though she managed to get one leg free, she was struggling to get her hands and other leg free. She wasn't getting anywhere. She began to think about her son Ivan and how she may not see him again. Ivy began to cry. Then she thought to herself, "Brazil knows I will never just leave my son. He will be looking for me for sure. I need to try something different to get free but what?" Ivy began to think as she continued to get her arms free. Then she stopped and said to herself, "I know what I can try. I sure hope it works." Ivy no longer tried to free herself. She was waiting for Malena to return.

Dr. Baker's Office

Brazil: Dr. Baker, are you okay?

Brazil had Ivan in one arm asleep and had his other hand out for a handshake. Dr. Baker was amazed by the resemblance between him and Mystery.

Brazil: Dr. Baker?

Dr. Baker: Oh yes, yes I'm fine. Forgive me.

Dr. Baker shook his hand. "You can lay Ivan down over there on the sofa."

Brazil laid him down.

Brazil: I take it by your reaction you know my twin brother.

Dr. Baker: I do. Mystery is a fine young man. As for you, it's finally good to put a name with a face. I've heard a lot about you. Now how can I help you?

Brazil: I'm sorry to stop by unexpected, but I needed to ask you something.

Dr. Baker: What is it?

Brazil: Have you seen or spoken to Ivy?

Dr. Baker: No, I haven't not since the other day. I've been here at the hospital working doubles. Is there something wrong?

Brazil: I'm beginning to think so.

Dr. Baker: Why would you say that?

Brazil: Ivy left Ivan with a babysitter yesterday early evening and never came back to pick him up, and she never called. The babysitter called me today to come get him. She said she had tried calling Ivy several times but there was no answer.

Dr. Baker: That's not like Ivy at all.

Brazil: I know. I tried calling her too, but it goes straight to voice mail.

Dr. Baker lifted his finger and said, "One second."

The doctor picked up his cell phone to call Ivy.

Dr. Baker: (Looking at Brazil.) Straight to the voice mail.

Dr. Baker hung the phone up. He instantly made another call.

Malik: Hello?

Dr. Baker: Hey, son, are you still here at the hospital.

Malik: Yes, I'm out here in the parking lot.

Dr. Baker: I need you to come back by my office before you leave.

Malik: Okay, I'm on my way back inside.

Dr. Baker: Alright.

They both hung up. Dr. Baker then addressed Brazil.

Dr. Baker: My son will be here in a few minutes. He works with the police force.

Brazil: That's good because I'm starting to get worried.

Dr. Baker: You and me both.

ALEXANDRIA'S ROOM

Dr. Walker showed Adriana and Max to Alexandria's room.

Dr. Walker: Here you go. Let Alexandria know that I will be back to check on her.

Adriana: Okay, thanks, Doctor.

Adriana and Max went in.

Adriana: Hey, sis.

Alexandria: Hey, you guys.

Adriana: I must say you look way better now than you did when we first brought you in.

They all laughed.

Alexandria: Max, you can lay Jase here next to me since he is asleep.

Max laid him down.

Alexandria: Did Dr. Walker tell you both about the baby?

Adriana: Yes, he did and we are so happy for you.

Max: Congratulations, Alexandria.

Alexandria: (Looking worried.) Thanks.

Adriana: Why are you looking so down? You should be happy right now. I know Jase is going to be thrilled when he wakes up and you tell him.

Alexandria: (Rubbing on Jase's back.) I know he will.

Adriana: Well, what's wrong?

Alexandria: I am worried about how Armon's going to take the news when he finds out.

Adriana: Girl, he already knows.

Alexandria: What do mean he already knows?

Adriana: Armon was with us when we brought you here. Unfortunately, Dr. Walker thought you both were happily married and told him he was going to be a father.

Alexandria: What!

Adriana: Long story short, he got upset and stormed out of the waiting room. We don't know where he went.

Alexandria: Oh no.

Max: You don't worry about him. He is a big boy. You have a new baby coming that you need to focus on now.

Adriana: Alexandria, who is the father of your baby?

Alexandria: His name is Brazil, and yes, before you ask, we have been seeing each other for a while now. Jase even knows him.

Adriana: Seriously, how are you going to keep this from me? Anyway, it doesn't matter, give me his number.

Alexandria: For what?

Adriana: Because I am going to call him to let him know you are in here. You need to tell him about the baby. Also, Max and I needs to go back home to Florida just for a few days to take care some things.

Max: (Looking confused.) We are?

Adriana: Yes, baby, you've forgotten already. Anyway, Alexandria, while we are gone, you need your new man to look after you, especially since Armon knows about your pregnancy.

Alexandria: You're right, but you guys hurry back.

Adriana: We will.

Alexandria gave her Brazil's number. She then gave Jase a kiss.

Max picked Jase up and they left the room. When they got in the hall, Max said, "Honey, are we really going to Florida?"

Adriana with tears in her eyes said, "Yes. I need to go see him and I need you there with me."

Max now understood.

Max: Oh, okay, I understand now. Of course I will be there with you.

Max and Adriana left the hospital.

On the next episode, Brazil gets the bad news about Mystery.

Episode 12

Brazil and Dr. Baker was talking when there was a knock at the door.

Dr. Baker: Come in.

It was Malik.

Dr. Baker: Hey, son, I'm glad I caught you before you left. This is Brazil, Ivy's ex-husband.

Malik, shocked by the resemblance, said, "You look like . . ."

Brazil interrupted him. "Mystery? He's my twin brother."

Malik was surprised because he never knew Mystery had a twin. They both shook hands.

Malik: Good to meet you.

Brazil: Likewise.

Dr. Baker: Son, have you seen or heard from your sister?

Malik: She came by the house last night, but I had to work so I left her there with Malena.

Dr. Baker: You haven't heard from her since?

Malik: No. Is there something wrong?

Brazil: She is missing.

Malik: What do you mean she's missing?

Brazil: She left Ivan at a playmates early yesterday evening and didn't call or go back to pick him up. He stayed the night there. The babysitter called me a few hours ago, and I went and got him. I have called and left voice mails for her, but she hasn't responded or anything.

Dr. Baker: Son, can you call Malena and see if she's still there?

Malik: Sure, hold on.

Malik took out his cell and called home to Malena.

Malena: Hello?

Malik: Hey, babe.

Malena: Hey, are you on your way home?

Malik: Not yet, but I need to ask you something.

Malena: Okay.

Malik: Is Ivy still there with you. I know I left her there last night.

Malena thought about what Armon told her to say. She was nervous.

Malena: (Nervous.) No, no, honey. She left here late last night. Is there something wrong?

Malik: I hope not but we think she may be missing. I will talk to you when I get home. I need to put a search out for her. Talk to you later, love you.

Malik hung up, not giving Malena chance to say "I love you" back.

Malik: Okay, I'm going back to the station to start a missing person report on her and to put a BOLO out on her car.

Dr. Baker: I pray everything is okay.

Brazil: Me too.

Malik: Dad, I'm going to find my sister no matter what it takes.

Brazil: If I can do anything to help, let me know. She means a lot to me.

Malik: I will let you know. Dad, everything is going to be okay. I promise.

Malik left.

Brazil: Guess I will be going too.

Dr. Baker: Wait, Brazil, I need to tell you something.

MASON'S ROOM

The nurse was in with Mason taking his blood pressure and changing his IV bag.

Nurse: How are you feeling?

Mason: Like I've been run over by a truck.

The nurse laughed.

Nurse: It's going to take some time, but you will get better. It's now all about letting your body heal itself. You're a lucky man.

Mason: Yea, I know.

Nurse: Is there anything I can get for you before I go?

Mason: No, thanks.

The nurse turned to leave.

Mason: Nurse?

Nurse: Yes?

Mason: Can you hand me the phone?

"Sure," said the nurse. The nurse handed him the phone. "Anything else?"

Mason: What room number is this?

Nurse: 330.

Mason: Okay, thanks. That will be all.

The nurse said "okay" then left the room.

Mason made a call but had to leave a voice mail.

Mason: Hey, it's me, Mason. I have never asked you for anything my whole life, but now I need your help. I'm at Emory Hospital, room 330. I need you to come get me.

DR. BAKER'S OFFICE

Brazil: What you need to tell me?

Dr. Baker: Mystery had a terrible accident last night and had to be admitted here.

Brazil: What? What happened? Is he going to be okay?

Dr. Baker: I don't know yet. He fell from a fourth-floor apartment building.

Brazil: What? Are you serious?

Dr. Baker: I'm afraid so. He ruptured both his kidneys, so I had to do emergency surgery to stop the internal bleeding. Now I haven't had the chance to call your mother yet. I can do that while you go see him if you want.

Brazil: Yes, please call her. She is going to be devastated.

Dr. Baker: I will do that now. Mystery is in room 348. Ivan can stay here until you come back.

Brazil: Thank you.

Brazil left the office to go to his brother.

The doctor sat down at his desk and call Diane. Diane was at Mystery's house watching television when her cell phone rang. She saw it was the doctor.

Diane: Hey, Joshua.

Dr. Baker: Diane, I need you to come to the hospital as soon as possible. It's Mystery.

Diane sat up straight in the chair.

Diane: What's wrong with Mystery?

Dr. Baker: I rather explained it to you when you get here.

Diane: I'm leaving now.

Diane hung up, got her keys and coat, and ran out the house. She got in the car and sped off. An unknown vehicle cut their lights on and followed her.

On the season finale, Mystery wakes up.

Episode 13

Brazil made it to Mystery's room. When he went in, he saw Clay sitting, there holding his hand. Clay stood up.

Clay: Oh, hey, Brazil.

Brazil: (Looking at Mystery laying there.) How is he?

Clay: He's been like this since I've been here. My dad has him sedated.

Brazil looked at Clay. He saw how his face looked.

Brazil: Are you okay?

Clay: (Dropping his head.) Yea, I'll be fine just ready for Mystery to wake up. Look, I'm going to leave and give you some time along with your brother.

Brazil: You don't have to leave.

Clay: It's okay. I need to go see someone anyways. I won't be long.

Brazil: Okay then.

Clay left the room. Brazil sat down by the bed.

Brazil: Okay, bro. I need you to wake up.

MASON'S ROOM

Clay went to Mason's room. He was outside the door debating on whether to go in or not. He knew he would have to face him at some point. He built up the nerves to go in. When he went inside, he saw that Mason wasn't there. The nurse came in.

Clay: Excuse me, nurse. Do you know where Mason is?

The nurse, looking confused, said, "No, I don't and it's time for his medicine." The nurse knocked on the bathroom door. "Mason, are you in there?" There was no answer.

Clay: Could his doctor have taken him for more testing or something?

Nurse: I don't think he was schedule for testing. Let me look at his chart.

The nurse pulled his chart from the bottom of the bed.

Nurse: It doesn't show that testing was scheduled. Something is not right here.

Clay: Could he have left on his own.

Nurse: That's not possible. He was strapped to the bed to keep him from moving. Mind you, he also has a cast on his arm and leg.

The nurse hit the emergency button. Two other nurses ran to the room.

Nurse: Someone find Dr. Spencer and call security. Let them know we have a missing patient somewhere in the hospital.

Clay walked out of the room, nervous. All kinds of thoughts rushed to his head. He felt in his bones that Mason had left the hospital. He knew as long as Mason was out there, he would never be safe. Clay knew he would have to watch over his shoulder because he knew Mason would want revenge.

DR. BAKER'S OFFICE

Diane made it to the hospital. She ran to Dr. Baker's office. When she got there, she just bust in without knocking. She didn't even realize that Ivan, her grandson, was on the sofa, asleep. The doctor was sitting at his desk.

Diane: (Hysterical.) What happened to my boy?

The doctor stood up and came from around the desk. "Calm down and have a seat."

Diane: I don't want to sit down. I want to know what happened to my son. Where is he?

Dr. Baker: I have him sedated. Diane, he was one of the boys that fell from that fourth-floor apartment balcony yesterday.

Diane just covered her mouth and started to cry. "Oh my God."

Facing Diane, the doctor grabbed both of her arms to comfort.

Dr. Baker: He fell on his back puncturing both of his kidneys. When the ambulance made it here with him, he was unconscious and had serious internal bleeding. We had to do emergency surgery to stop it and to repair his kidneys.

Diane: (Crying.) That's my baby. I can't lose my baby. I just got him back.

Dr. Baker: You're not going to lose him. We need to wait and see to make sure the repairs is enough for his kidneys to function on their own. If not he will need a kidney transplant. I'm hoping for the best.

Diane: I need to see him. Take me to him.

Dr. Baker: Sure come with me.

Dr. Baker escorted Diane to Mystery's room. Before she opened the door to go in, she took a deep breath. The doctor was right there with her. Diane opened the door and they went in. Diane covered her mouth when she saw Mystery lying there unconscious. She looked over and saw Brazil sitting there. Brazil came to her to hug her. She started to cry.

Brazil: I just found out myself.

Diane went and sat down on the bed beside Mystery. She took his hands in hers.

Dr. Baker: I will leave you two along with him.

Dr. Baker left the room. Brazil went and stood behind his mother.

Diane: Hey, baby, it's Diane. Its Mom. I'm here. I came as soon as I heard. I need you to fight, baby, okay. I need you to wake up.

Diane was holding his hand to her face.

Diane: Brazil, how did this happen?

Brazil: I don't know. The doctor didn't go into detail with me.

Diane: (Angry.) I need to find out. I don't believe for one second he just fell. Someone is going to pay for this.

At the Hotel

Max and Adriana went back to the hotel to pack a few things for their trip back home to Florida. They planned to return in a few days.

Max: Baby, are you okay? You didn't say anything all the way here. Talk to me.

Adriana: I'm okay. Finding out Alexandria fixing to have another child just got me to thinking about him that's all. You know it's his birthday this week?

Max: Ohhhhhhh, that's right.

Adriana: So now you understand why I need to go and visit my son?

Max: Of course, baby. Of course.

Malik's House

After Malena hung up with Malik, she went to go check on Ivy. She went down to the basement. When she got to the door, she noticed that she forgot to lock it back. "You have to be more careful, Malena," she said to herself. She went inside.

Ivy: Malena, I can't feel my hands. You have this tape too tight. It is cutting the blood circulation off to my hands. Please take them off.

Malena: You know I can't do that.

Ivy: Malena, I don't want to lose my hands behind all this nonsense. Please. You can re-tape them again, just not so tight. I have to use the bathroom anyway or do you want me to just go right here in my clothes?

Malena: Okay, okay, one second.

Malena left the room.

Ivy: Where are you going?

Malena went back upstairs to the kitchen. She grabbed a knife and scissors, then she went back to the storage room where she was keeping Ivy.

Malena: Okay, I am going to cut the tapes off and let you go to the bathroom. There is one right outside. We never use it but it's usable.

Ivy: Thank you.

Malena cut the tape from one of her legs. She noticed that Ivy had bust through the other one. Malena stood up holding up the knife. "When I cut your hands loose, don't try anything, okay? I don't want to hurt you."

Ivy: Okay, I won't.

Malena proceeded to cut the tape off both her hands. Ivy began moving her hands and wiggling her fingers to get the blood flowing. As she stood up, Malena backed away slowly, holding the knife straight out.

Ivy: Ahhhhhh, that feels better. Thank you.

Ivy started to stretch and turned her back to Malena.

Malena: The bathroom is this way.

Ivy: I know. I just needed to stretch.

Ivy saw a thick hard back book on one of the boxes.

Malena: Let's go, Ivy.

Ivy picked up the book. She turned around quick and threw it at Malena's face. Then she lunged for Malena. Malena blocked her face, but the book knocked the knife out of her hands. Before she knew it, Ivy was on her. Ivy pushed her over the two bicycles that were in there. Although Ivy wanted to hurt Malena, she just ran out of the storage room, closed and locked the door behind her. Malena got up and tried to get out but couldn't. She yelled out, "Ivy open the door please. I'm sorry."

Ivy just stood there. She looked around and tried to get her thoughts together, then she ran up the stairs, went through the kitchen to the front door. When she opened it, Armon was standing there, fixing to knock.

Armon: Well, where are you going in such a hurry?

JACKSON'S CONDO

Mason: I want to thank you for helping me leave the hospital.

Jackson: Well, you made it sound like a life-or-death situation.

Mason: Almost.

Jackson: Look, Mason, I don't know what you have gotten yourself into, but I am not going to be a part of it. I mean, what if Jo Jo, or Dr. Baker to you, saw me wheeling you out the hospital.

Mason: Well, no one did. I mean look at you. You wore a hoodie.

Jackson: That's not the point. Anything could have happened. Also you can't stay here with me.

Mason: Where am I going to go?

Jackson: That's not my problem. I've helped you this far.

Mason: (Getting angry.) You mean to tell me you're going to throw me out on the streets when you know I can't walk or even stand. What kind of father are you?

MYSTERY'S ROOM

Brazil was looking out the window. Diane was still sitting by Mystery, holding his hand. Brazil realized that his mom hadn't move since she got here.

Brazil: Mom, you okay? You want me to get you something to drink?

Diane: Yes, please, some water, baby. Thank you.

Brazil started out the door when Diane stopped him.

Diane: (Excited.) Brazil, wait.

Brazil: What is it, Mom?

Diane: Mystery just squeezed my hand.

Brazil walked over to the bed to see.

Diane: (Laughing.) See, see, he did it again. Did you see it?

Brazil: Yes, I saw it. He's waking up. Look at his eyes.

Mystery's eye lids were moving. He started to grunt.

Diane: Go get the doctor quick.

Brazil ran out of the room to go get Dr. Baker.

Diane: That's right, baby, wake up. Wake up for me.

Mystery was grunting more and breathing heavily. A few minutes later, Brazil came back with Dr. Baker. Brazil stayed outside because his phone had rang. Dr. Baker went on inside.

Diane: Joshua, I believe he is waking up.

Dr. Baker: Mystery? Mystery can you hear me?

Diane: Joshua, why is he grunting like that? Is he in pain?

Dr. Baker: He may be feeling some discomfort but that is normal. Let me check his blood pressure.

The doctor checked Mystery's blood pressure.

Dr. Baker: It's a little high, but I can get that down. Mystery, open your eyes for us. Can you do that?

Mystery was blinking his eyes really fast. He was grunting and breathing hard.

Diane: Come on, baby.

Dr. Baker: Take your time. Don't rush it.

Mystery opened his eyes slowly. The light was so bright to him. He had to give his eyes some time to adjust. When he did, he looked around.

Mystery confused and barely getting the words out said, "Where am I?"

Dr. Baker: You're at Emory Hospital.

Mystery: (Grunting.) Hospital?

Dr. Baker: Yes. You gave us quite a scare.

Mystery looked around and saw Diane standing there.

Mystery: Doc, who is this woman?

To be continued . . .

PART 5

Episode 1

Max and Adriana had finally gotten on the road headed to Florida with Jase. She decided to call Brazil. His phone rang.

Brazil: Hello, this is Brazil.

Adriana: Hello, Brazil. This is Adriana. I'm Alexandria's sister.

Brazil: Oh, hey, how are you? I've heard a lot about you.

Adriana: Wish I could say the same about you. I am calling you to let you know Alexandria is in the hospital at Emory.

Brazil: What? Is she okay?

Adriana: Yes, she is going to fine. She has a bad case of the flu. My husband and I got her there in time before it got any worst.

Brazil: Oh man, I told her she needed to see the doctor earlier. I am actually at Emory right now. What room number is she in?

Adriana: She's in room 540. Brazil, one last thing.

Brazil: What is it?

Adriana: My husband and I are heading out of town and will be back in a couple days. Can you keep check on her while we are gone? Her crazy husband is in town and is upset with her right now. We just don't want her to be alone.

Brazil knew Adriana was talking about Armon. He still felt bad about letting him know Alexandria was in Atlanta.

Brazil: I am headed to her right now and will stay with her. Thanks for letting me know.

Adriana: You're welcome.

They both hung up.

MYSTERY'S ROOM

Mystery: Doctor, who is this woman?

Dr. Baker and Diane looked at each other. Mystery turned to look at Diane.

Mystery: Lady, who are you. Why are you here?

Diane: Mystery, it's me Diane. Your mo—

Before Diane could finish saying "mother," Dr. Baker held his hand up for her to stop.

Dr. Baker: Mystery? Do you not recognize this lady?

Mystery: No, I don't. Should I? Where is my mom? Where is Gloria?

Diane was stunned by what she was witnessing.

Dr. Baker: Diane, can I speak with you in the hall, please?

Diane: (Confused.) Sure.

Dr. Baker: Mystery, I will be right back, okay, buddy?

Dr. Baker and Diane left the room.

Diane: What is happening?

Dr. Baker: It looks like Mystery has suffered some memory lost. That is not uncommon for that to happen to patients that have had an accident like he did.

Diane: He doesn't know who I am.

Dr. Baker: I know. Let me go back in and talk to him. Then I will how bad it is.

Diane: (Upset.) Okay.

Dr. Baker went back into the room. An unknown person was watching Diane as she waited outside the room.

JACKSON'S CONDO

Jackson: What did you just say to me? Don't think you're going to talk to me any kind of way and disrespect me in my own house.

Mason: I wasn't trying to do that. I just don't understand how you can just turn your back on your own son again. Dad, I need you right now.

Jackson: Mason, you know the kind of relationship we've had all your life. That hasn't change. I still feel the same way.

Mason: Oh, that's right. You never wanted kids, and it was all my mother's fault that she got pregnant with me, right?

Jackson: I never said that, but she knew how I felt about the situation.

Mason: (His voice raising.) Situation. Situation. I wasn't a situation. I was your son. I am your son. You do know you are the reason my mom is dead.

Jackson just stood there in shock.

MALIK'S HOUSE

Armon: Well, where are you going in such a hurry?

Ivy, not knowing who Armon really was, just fell into his arms crying.

Ivy: (Hysterical.) Please help me. I need to leave here now. Please.

Armon: (Grabbing Ivy by the arms gently.) Calm down. I will help you.

Ivy: (Scared and looking over her shoulder.) We have to leave now.

Armon: I'm sorry about this.

Ivy: (Confused.) Huh, sorry about what?

Armon punched Ivy in the face, knocking her out. She fell to the floor. Armon picked her up in his arms, closed the door behind him, and headed back to the basement.

On the next episode, Alexandria tells Brazil he's going to be a father.

Episode 2

Dr. Baker went back into the room.

Mystery: Doc, I want to see my mom.

Dr. Baker: I need to check you out first and make sure everything is okay. You've had a terrible accident.

Dr. Baker pulled up a rolling stool beside the bed.

Dr. Baker: Now I need to ask you a few questions.

Mystery: Okay.

Dr. Baker: Do you know what happened to you?

Mystery: No.

Dr. Baker: You fell from a fourth-floor balcony.

Mystery: (Looking confused.) Are you serious?

Dr. Baker: I'm afraid so. Do you know where you were today before this happened?

Mystery: (Trying to remember.) No, I don't. Doc, what is happening to me? Why can't I remember?

Dr. Baker: This is not uncommon. I'm going to have to run more test on you to see how severe this is. Now just a few more questions. Mystery, are you sure you don't know anything about the lady that was just in here?

Mystery, getting frustrated because he can't remember anything, said, "No, I told you."

Dr. Baker: Do you know Brazil?

Mystery: Who? No. I do not.

Dr. Baker: What year is it?

Mystery: (Now angry.) What year is it? What kind of question is that? It's 2010.

Dr. Baker paused because it was 2015. Mystery had lost his memory for the last five years.

Dr. Baker: Okay, I don't have any more questions. I am going to have the nurses come get you in a little bit for more testing. I need to do an MRI on your brain, okay?

Mystery: Okay, that's fine. Now can you contact my mom for me?

Dr. Baker: I will do that. You just lay here and rest, okay, buddy?

Dr. Baker left the room.

JACKSON'S CONDO

Jackson: How are you going to say something like that? I am not the reason your mom died.

Mason: Yes, you are. She drank herself to death after you left her. She was in love with you and you broke her heart. You just up and leave her with a young child to raise.

Jackson: Mason—

Mason: Don't Mason me. You know what the sad part is?

Jackson just stood there. Mason continued.

Mason: She never talked bad about you. She never tried to turn me against you not once. She loved you to the very end.

Jackson: I loved her too, Mason. And believe it or not, I love you too.

Mason: (Laughing.) Please.

Jackson: I do.

Mason: You know I was thirteen when my mom died. I remember child protective services telling me that I had to go to a foster home. I ran away and came to you looking for a place to stay, looking for my father to help me. You know what you did?

Jackson: Mason—

Mason cut him off. "You turned your back on me. You told me that you had too much going on to look after a child and you closed the door in my face. You did that to me."

Jackson: Mason, I was young back then.

Mason: So was my mother. You are the reason I turned out to be the man I am today.

Jackson: What does that mean?

ALEXANDRIA'S ROOM

Brazil made it to Alexandria's room. He knocked lightly and stuck his head in the door. He saw she was asleep. Brazil went on in. He stood there watching her sleep. She looked so beautiful to him. He was really happy to have her in his life and would do anything to protect her. He knew he needed to be honest and tell her that Armon was in town because of him. Alexandria started to wake up. She turned her head and saw Brazil standing there. She was so happy to see him.

Brazil: Hey, you.

Alexandria: Hey. How long have you been standing there?

Brazil: Not long. Your sister called me and told me you was here. How are you feeling?

Alexandria: Much better.

Brazil gave her a kiss on the forehead. He decided to go ahead and tell her about bringing Armon to Atlanta.

Brazil: Alexandria, there is something I need to tell you.

Alexandria, putting both hands on his face and smiling, said, "I have something to tell you to. I'm pregnant."

Brazil: What?

MALIK'S HOUSE

Armon carried Ivy back to the basement. He could hear Malena banging on the door, yelling for help. He laid Ivy on the floor, unlocked the storage room door, and opened it. Malena was relieved to see him instead of Malik. She didn't know how she would ever explain it if it was Malik. Malena ran into her brother's arms.

Malena: Armon, I'm so glad it's you.

Armon: Malena, what happened?

Malena, looking angry at Ivy lying on the floor, said, "That bitch tricked me."

Armon: Let me get her back in there.

Armon picked Ivy up and put her back in the chair. He retaped both her legs and wrists again. "You have to be more careful Malena. You are lucky she ran into me and not Malik."

Malena: (Feeling relieved.) I know. Trust me it will not happen again.

Armon: Come on and let's go back upstairs. She's not going anywhere now.

Armon and Malena went back upstairs to the kitchen.

Malena: What are doing back here so late?

Armon: (With an attitude.) By the look of things, it's a good thing that I did. Your world was about to be destroyed.

Malena just stared at Armon.

Armon: I'm sorry, sis. I'm just angry right now.

Malena could tell something was wrong. "What's wrong?"

Armon: Alexandria is in the hospital.

Malena: What? What happened?

Armon: (Taking a deep breath and looking up at the ceiling.) She's pregnant. My filthy wife is pregnant.

Malena: Oh, Armon, I am sorry.

Armon: This whole time I have been looking for her and she's been with someone else.

Malena could see the anger in his eyes. "Armon?"

Armon: She is going to pay for this.

Armon stormed out and left.

Malena: (Yelling for him.) Armon, come back.

Malena knew when Armon got like this, something bad was about to happen.

On the next episode, Mason lashes out at Jackson.

Episode 3

As Dr. Baker left the room, Diane met him at the door.

Diane anxious to know said, "What happened?"

Dr. Baker: Calm down. Come to my office with me.

As they were fixing to leave, Clay walked up.

Clay: Dad, how is Mystery?

Dr. Baker: He is going to be okay. He can't have any visitors right now.

Diane: Joshua, this is your son?

Dr. Baker: Yes, he is my youngest. Have you two met?

Diane: Yes, we've met. Mystery introduced us. What happened to your face, baby?

Clay just dropped his head.

Dr. Baker: Both of you come with me to my office.

They both followed him to his office.

JACKSON'S CONDO

Jackson: What do you mean I am the reason you turned out to be the man you are.

Mason: Bitter and angry all the time.

Jackson: I'm sorry you feel that way.

Mason: Don't be sorry. I don't want your sympathy.

Jackson: What is it you want me to say?

Mason: Nothing. When you closed that door in my face that day, my whole life changed. I was not going to be put in a foster home so I ran away. I lived on the streets for years. Do you know what it's like growing up on these Atlanta streets? I was only a child.

Jackson could tell this was something that Mason had been holding in for years. He needed to get it off his chest so he let him.

Mason: I did whatever it took to survive. I stole, I robbed, sold drugs, anything you could think of. I did it. That is what your child had to do to survive in these streets while his father lived in luxury with no care in the world.

Jackson couldn't say anything. He felt and could see the hatred Mason had for him and he had every right to feel that way.

Mason continued. "I use to wait outside your condo in the dark, sometimes in the pouring rain just to watch you come home, pull up in your fancy Mercedes truck with a different woman every time, living the good life."

Jackson: Mason, look, I'm sorry.

Mason: Like I said I don't want your sympathy. I will be out of here tomorrow as soon as possible.

Jackson: Mason—

Mason: Just leave me alone.

Jackson didn't say anything else. He left the room and gave Mason his space.

ALEXANDRIA'S ROOM

Brazil: Wait a minute. Did I hear you right?

Alexandria: (Laughing.) Yes. We are going to have a baby.

Brazil was overjoyed. "Oh, baby, that's wonderful news." He leaned over and gave her a deep, passionate kiss. "I can't tell you how happy you have made me right now." He kissed her again.

Alexandria: I love you.

Brazil: I love you too. So what did the doctor say? Is everything okay with the baby?

Alexandria: Everything is fine. He is letting me go home tomorrow. Granted I have to take several medication now.

Brazil: And I am going to make sure you do. You are living for two now.

Brazil laid his head on her stomach and closed his eyes. He was so happy. Alexandria rubbed his head.

Alexandria: So what was it you needed to tell me?

Brazil slowly opened his eyes.

DR. BAKER'S OFFICE

When Dr. Baker, Diane, and Clay got to his office and went in, Diane noticed Ivan was there asleep.

Diane: What is my grandson doing here? I didn't even notice he was here when I first got here.

Dr. Baker: He's here with Brazil. I told Brazil he can lay in here while he visited Mystery. Now I want you both to have seat.

Diane and Clay both sat down.

Dr. Baker: (Addressing Diane.) Diane, you are considered Mystery's next of kin even though he doesn't remember you right now.

Clay: (Interrupting.) Dad, what do you mean he doesn't remember her?

Dr. Baker: One second, Clay. Diane I need your permission to talk about Mystery's health and condition in front of Clay. This is a hospital policy.

Diane: (Looking at Clay). Yes it's ok. I know how much he means to my son.

Clay: Thank you.

Dr. Baker: Okay. Mystery is suffering from amnesia or memory loss. I don't know how severe it is or how long it will last. I am having the nurse prep him for more tests as we speak. I will know more after the test.

Diane: Can we see him?

Dr. Baker: I know you don't want to hear this, but I don't think that will be a good idea.

Diane: I don't understand. What is it you're not telling me?

Dr. Baker: Mystery has lost the last five years of his life. In his mind, he doesn't know you. He still thinks Gloria is his mother and that she is alive.

Diane: Oh no.

Clay: Dad, does he know us?

Dr. Baker: Yes, he remembers us because he has been knowing us and our family all his life. Now I need to ask you, Clay, what kind of relationship did you and Mystery have five years ago?

Clay: We didn't have a relationship. We didn't even look at each other like that. You remember he used to come by the house with . . .

Clay remembered something.

Clay: Oh no.

Dr. Baker: What is it, son?

Clay: Five years ago Mystery, Malik, and Mason were still the best of friends.

Diane: Is that a bad thing?

Clay: It is now. Mason is partly the reason Mystery is in here.

Diane: (Standing up.) What?

On the next episode, Dr. Baker finds out that Mason has left the hospital.

Episode 4

Diane: Clay, what do you mean this Mason person is the reason for Mystery being in here.

Clay: Mason and Mystery was fighting at my apartment.

Dr. Baker: Clay.

Clay: It's okay, Dad. I need to tell her the whole truth.

Diane: Then tell me. Why were they fighting in the first place?

Clay: They were fighting because of me.

Diane: What does that mean?

Clay: Mason is my ex-boyfriend. Do you remember the day Mystery introduced us?

Diane: Yes, it was the day of my sister's funeral. I walked in on you both in Mystery's room.

Clay: Well, that day, Mystery and I decided to work on getting back together. He told me that I had to break up with Mason first. Needless to say, when I tried to break it off with him, he did this to me. (Clay pointed at his swollen face.)

Clay: (Crying.) He beat me. He choked me. He kicked me and kept stomping me until I was unconscious.

Diane eyes started to fill with tears. Dr. Baker comforted his son by rubbing him on the back.

Dr. Baker: It's okay, son.

Clay: Somehow when I came to, I found myself at Mystery's front door. It's all still blur but I remembering lying in his lap while he cleaned my face. They next thing I remember was waking up and reading this letter he left me.

Diane: Letter?

Clay: A letter basically saying he couldn't let this go. I knew he was going to my place to confront Mason. By the time I made it there and got into the apartment, they were going over the balcony.

Clay was crying harder at this point.

Clay: I tried to get there in time. I never meant for any of this to happen.

Diane hugged him.

Diane: It's okay. Everything is going to be okay. Where is this Mason guy?

Dr. Baker: He's here as well.

Clay: No, he's not.

Dr. Baker: What do you mean, son?

Clay: He has left the hospital.

JACKSON'S CONDO

Jackson needed to go check on one of his bars downtown so he had to let Mason know he was leaving for a little while. He went to the guest room Mason was sleeping in for the time being. The door was half opened. He saw Mason just sitting there, staring out the window. Jackson knocked and went on in.

Jackson: Mason, I need to step out for a little while. Are you okay? Do you need anything before I go?

Mason, not even turning around, said, "Don't you worry about me. I'll be fine. Go take care of your priorities."

Jackson: Mason?

Mason: I said I'm fine.

Jackson: Okay, okay, well, if you need me, you have my cell number.

Mason didn't respond, just continued on staring out the window. Jackson turned around and left.

ALEXANDRIA'S ROOM

Alexandria: What is it you needed to tell me?

Brazil wasn't about to tell her the truth about Armon now. He knew it would only upset her and he wasn't about to risk the health of her or their baby.

Brazil: It's not important now.

Alexandria: Are you sure?

Brazil: Yes, I'm sure. I don't want to think about anything right now but you and our baby.

As soon as he said that, the door slammed. Alexandria and Brazil both jumped. It was Armon.

On the next episode, Adriana visits her son.

Episode 5

Max and Adriana had made it back home to Florida. As soon as they got in town, they went straight to visit her son. Adriana had to build up her nerve before she got out to see him, so they both just sat in the car until she was ready. It had been a year since she last visited him, and it never got any easier for her.

Max: (Grabbing her hand.) Baby, it's okay. We can sit here as long as you like.

Adriana: Thank you. Just give me a few minutes.

Max: Of course.

They sat there for another five minutes. Then Adriana said, "I'm ready."

Max: Are you sure?

Adriana: Yes. Come on.

They got out of the car and headed to see her son. Jase was right there with them.

Jase: Where are we going?

Max: We're going to go see your cousin.

Jase: My cousin?

Max: Yes, your Aunt Adriana's son.

"There he is," Adriana said pointing. "Look at that perfect little face." Adrian got teary-eyed but started to talk to her son. "Hey, baby, it's Mom. Happy birthday. You know Mommy wasn't going to forget your birthday. I love you so much. There isn't a day that goes by that I don't think about you and wish you was with me. When you were born, you was the most precious thing to me and you still are. That will never change."

Adriana just stood there. Max and Jase were right there with her for support.

Adriana continued, "I hate to leave you so soon, but Mommy needs to get back to Atlanta and check on Aunt Alexandria, but before I go, I have a birthday gift for you. I hope you like it."

Adriana reached in her pocket book and pulled out a batman action figure and a red rose. She laid the rose and placed the action figure on her son's tombstone. The heart-shaped tombstone had a baby picture sketched on it and it read, "Rest in peace, Baby CJ. May the angels watch over you."

She kissed her hand and touched the tombstone. She turned to Max and said, "I'm ready." Then she walked back to the car. Max and Jase followed.

When they got back in the car, Max asked her, "Baby, are you okay?"

Adriana: I'll be fine. Today is always hard for me. It's CJ's birthday. He would have been the same age as you, Jase.

Jase: Why did he die?

Adriana: When he was born, he got sick in the hospital and never got better. He is in a better place now though. He's with Jesus in heaven.

Max started the car and they left.

Dr. Baker's Office

Dr. Baker: Clay, what do you mean he's left the hospital?

Clay: I went to his room to confront him, and he wasn't there. I asked the nurse and she said he wasn't scheduled for any kind of testing and that he should have been in bed. She called for security and informed his doctor that they had a missing patient.

Dr. Baker: It is impossible for him to leave the hospital with his conditions. He can't even walk.

Clay: Someone had to help him. I have a really bad feeling about this.

Dr. Baker: Let me called Dr. Spencer. He's Mason's doctor.

Dr. Baker called Dr. Spencer office. The phone rang.

Dr. Spencer: Dr. Spencer office.

Dr. Baker: Hey, Phil, it's Dr. Baker. Where is Mason?

Dr. Spencer: I was just about to call you. You need to meet me in the IT security department.

Dr. Baker: I will be right there.

They hung up.

Dr. Baker: Okay, I need to go see Dr. Spencer. I will find out what happened. Meanwhile, Diane, you can't visit Mystery right now okay? Not until I learn more about his memory lost. His conditions is very fragile and we don't want to upset him.

Diane: Okay, I understand.

Dr. Baker: Also you need to get in contact with Brazil and let him know as well. His face is the last face Mystery needs to see right now.

Diane: Okay, I will call him.

Dr. Baker: Clay, you can see him, but you can't let him know anything. Let him do the talking and you follow.

Clay: Okay, I promise.

Dr. Baker: Okay, I got to go.

Ivan was waking up from his nap.

Dr. Baker: Diane, can you watch Ivan?

Diane: Sure go ahead.

Dr. Baker left the office.

MALIK'S ROOM

Malena went to the basement to go check on Ivy. Malena open the door to the storage room and went in. Ivy was awake.

Malena: So you finally woke up?

Malena took the tape off of Ivy's mouth.

Ivy: Malena, you are going to go to jail for this. This is kidnapping.

Malena: I don't want to hear anything you have to say. You tried to trick me. Luckily, my brother caught you before you left.

Ivy: So that's who hit me. Do you really think you are going to get away with this?

Malena: I am doing what I have to do. I will not lose my husband.

Ivy: Malena, think about my son Ivan. I'm sure he is worried sick about me.

Malena: You will be back with him just as soon as I figured all this out.

Malena put the tape back on her mouth without giving her a chance to respond and left the room.

ALEXANDRIA'S ROOM

Alexandria and Brazil both jumped when they heard the door slammed. It was Armon. They hadn't even heard him come in until he closed the door. Armon had a serious look on his face. Brazil stood up and Alexandria sat up in the bed.

Armon: Am I interrupting something?

Alexandria: Armon, what are you doing here?

Armon: A husband can't come see his wife when she is in the hospital?

Alexandria: Don't do this here. You need to leave.

Armon hadn't even looked at Brazil the whole time. Brazil interrupted with his hand out looking for a handshake. "Hey, I'm Brazil."

Armon looked at him then down at his hand then back at his face again. Seeing that Armon wasn't going to shake hands, Brazil lowered his.

Armon: Who are you again?

Brazil: I'm Brazil. Alexandria's—

Before he could finish, Armon interrupted, "I need to talk to my wife alone if you don't mind."

Brazil looked at Alexandria.

Alexandria: It's okay.

Brazil: You sure?

Alexandria: Yes. Can you go check with Dr. Walker and see what time I can leave?

Brazil said okay, then left the room. Armon did not take his eyes off Alexandria as Brazil left the room.

Alexandria looked at Armon and said, "What do you want?"

On the next episode, Dr. Baker finds out who help Mason.

Episode 6

Dr. Baker met Dr. Spencer in the IT security office.

Dr. Spencer: Dr. Baker, there's something you need to see.

Dr. Baker: What is it?

Dr. Spencer: You know there is video surveillance setup throughout the hospital.

Dr. Baker: Yes.

Dr. Spencer: Well, Mason has left the hospital. We have him on tape leaving his room, then again outside in the parking lot.

Dr. Baker: That's impossible. He has a broken leg and hip.

Dr. Spencer: I know. He had help.

Dr. Baker: Are you serious?

Dr. Spencer: Yes, watch this.

Dr. Spencer instructed the IT clerk to start the video for Dr. Baker. The video clearly showed someone in a hoodie going into Mason's room with a wheelchair then about fifteen minutes later leaving the room with Mason.

"Okay, go to the next clip," Dr. Spencer said to the clerk.

The next clip showed the person pushing Mason down the hallway to the elevator.

Dr. Baker: Do anybody knows who that is?

Dr. Spencer: No the only thing we can make out on this video is the nice Rolex watch that he is wearing.

The clerk enlarged the video clip so Dr. Baker can see the watch clearer. Dr. Baker looked down at his own watch.

Dr. Spencer: It looks like the same exact watch you are wearing.

Dr. Baker: I see that. Wait a minute, you don't think I helped him out of here do you after what he did to my son?

Dr. Spencer: Of course not.

Dr. Baker: Good.

Dr. Spencer instructed the clerk to start the last video. This clip showed the guy in the hoodie pushing Mason to his truck and helping him get in, then taking off. Dr. Baker couldn't believe what he was seeing.

Dr. Baker: Wait, it that a Mercedes truck?

Dr. Spencer: Yes. Do you know who truck that is?

Dr. Baker: I'm not sure.

Dr. Spencer: If you know something, you need to let me know. Mason is my patient, and he will not survive with injuries like his especially with no medicine.

Dr. Baker: Don't you think I know that. Let me make some calls and see what I can find out. I will let you know as soon as I know something.

Dr. Baker left the room quickly. When he got to the hallway he had to stop and catch his breath.

Dr. Baker: (To himself.) That couldn't be. He wouldn't do that.

Dr. Baker made a call from his cell phone, but he got a voice mail.

Dr. Baker: Hey, this is Joshua. I'm at the hospital. I need to see you right now.

Dr. Baker hung up and went to wait in his office.

ALEXANDRIA'S ROOM

Alexandria: Armon, what do you want?

Armon: Where is my son?

Alexandria: He's with Max and my sister. Don't try to make it seem that you are here to see Jase. Let's just talk about what is really bothering you, the fact that I am pregnant with another man's child.

Armon: You say that so arrogantly.

Alexandria: I'm not being arrogant, Armon. I'm just happy. I never thought I would be able to have another child after Jase.

Armon: You are still my wife. How can you just lay down with another man?

Alexandria: Armon, I told you there was no chance we were getting back together. I've moved on.

Armon: With this Brazil character? Don't think for one second I will have another man raising my son.

Alexandria: You don't even know him.

Armon: Do you?

Alexandria: Yes, I do. He is a good man. He owns his own private investigation firm. He has a son almost the same age as Jase.

Armon: (Thinking.) Private investigator?

Alexandria: Yes, so.

Armon: (Anxious.) I need to go but this is not over by a long shot.

Armon nearly ran out of the room. As soon as he got outside, he ran back into Brazil.

On the next episode, Armon figures out who Brazil really is.

Episode 7

Armon: Brazil, is it?

Brazil: That's right.

Armon: Can I talk to you for a minute in the waiting room?

Brazil: (Answering slowly.) Sure.

They both walked to the waiting room.

Brazil: What is it you want to talk to me about?

Armon: I'm just going to be straightforward with you. So you are the one who knocked up my wife?

Brazil: I mean, I wouldn't put it like that. We have been together for a while now.

Armon: But she is my wife, you do know that, right?

Brazil: Look, I don't have any problems with you. I think you should be having this conversation with her but what I can tell you is that we are together and I am not going anywhere.

Armon: Oh, really.

Brazil: That's right.

Armon: You know I don't know many guys whose name is Brazil. Hell, honestly I don't know any guys with that name. It's a very rare and unique name.

Brazil: What are you getting at?

Armon: It didn't dawn on me who you really were until Alexandria told me you were a private investigator.

Brazil froze.

Armon: Then I realize, you are the same private investigator that helped me find my Alexandria. Now I have a question for you. Do she know you are the reason I am here in Atlanta?

DR. BAKER'S OFFICE

Dr. Baker was sitting in his office when there was a knock on his door.

Dr. Baker: Come in.

It was Jackson. Jackson came in and gave his friend a hug.

Jackson: Hey, buddy. Is everything okay? You sounded strange on the phone.

Dr. Baker: I needed to talk to you about something. It's very important.

Jackson: What is it? Is it about Kennedy? Is he okay?

Dr. Baker: Kennedy's fine.

Dr. Baker: (Taking a deep breath.) It's about you.

Jackson: What about me?

Dr. Baker: I need to ask you something, and I need you to be completely honest with me.

Jackson: Okay, well, ask me.

Dr. Baker: Did you help a patient leave the hospital yesterday?

Jackson was almost not surprised by the question. He had a feeling that he was seen when he were helping Mason leave the hospital. He wasn't going to lie to his friend. It was obvious to Jackson that Joshua knew. He just needed confirmation. Jackson looked up at the ceiling and took a deep breath and said, "Yes."

On the next episode, Jackson and Dr. Baker argue.

Episode 8

Armon: Do Alexandria know you are the reason I am here in Atlanta?

Brazil didn't say anything. He was speechless.

Armon: By the look on your face right now and the fact that you are speechless tells me she doesn't. I wonder what she will say when she finds out.

Brazil: She's not going to find out.

Armon: Oh, so you plan on keeping this from her. Keeping secrets already, are you?

Brazil: Look, I am bound by a confidentiality clause to my clients and my clients are bound to. You should know that. You signed the document.

Armon: You think I give a dam about some paperwork. Obviously, you don't know me very well.

Brazil: You will be breaking the law if you tell her anything.

Armon: (Laughing.) I am the law and I have people in very high places.

Brazil: Look, why are you doing this. It's obvious that Alexandria has moved on. Why can't you let her be?

Armon: I will never let her be. She is my wife. We made vows. We have a son together. You think I'm going to let someone else raise my child.

Brazil started to say something else but Armon interrupted.

Armon: You have one of two options. You can tell Alexandria the truth, or I will.

Armon left the waiting room not giving Brazil a chance to say anything. Brazil couldn't believe he was put in this situation. He left the waiting room and went back to Alexandria's room. When he went in, she was asleep. He sat down in the chair next to the bed and watched her slept.

DR. BAKER'S OFFICE

Jackson: Yes, it was me. Something is telling me that you already knew though.

Dr. Baker: I wasn't completely sure, but I am glad you are being honest with me.

Jackson: How did you find out? I know there are cameras throughout the hospital, but I wore a hoodie to make sure I couldn't be recognized.

Dr. Baker: I recognized your watch on the video. Then I saw your truck leave the parking lot after you helped him get in. Why would you do this?

Jackson: What do you mean?

Dr. Baker: Help someone you don't even know.

Jackson: I know him.

Dr. Baker: How do you know him? Do you know what that punk did?

Jackson: Whoa, why are you getting so upset? What did he do that is so bad?

Dr. Baker: He beat up Clay. That's what he did.

Jackson: (Shocked.) What?

Dr. Baker: Yes, he beat up my son.

Jackson: Josh, I didn't know that trust me. How is Clay? Is he okay?

Dr. Baker: He's going to be fine. His face is all swollen and bruised though.

Jackson: If I had known that had happened, I would have never helped Mason.

Dr. Baker: Why would you, Jackson?

Jackson: It's complicated.

Dr. Baker: Complicated? Did he even tell you how he got here?

Jackson: No, and I didn't ask.

Dr. Baker: Well, let me explain it to you since you are in the business of helping total strangers.

Jackson: He's not a stran—

Dr. Baker cut him off. "Mason and Clay were boyfriends. They were in a relationship. Mason was abusing Clay for quite a while from what I gather. Clay got up the nerve to finally tell Mason it was over and that he was going back to his ex and Mason beat him up for it."

Jackson: Well, how did Mason end up in here.

Dr. Baker: Clay's ex confronted Mason and they fought. During the fight, they both managed to go over a balcony four stories up.

Jackson was totally surprised by all this.

Jackson: Wow, I hate that happened.

Dr. Baker: You hate it for whom, Clay or your new friend?

Jackson: Come on, Joshua, don't do that. I hate it for all involved. You know I love Clay like he was my own child
.

Dr. Baker: You have a funny way of showing it.

Jackson was starting to get irritated by the slick remarks Joshua was making. He raised his voice and said, "What's with all the slick comments. Why are you being confrontational with me right now?"

Dr. Baker raised his voice back, "How could you help a loser like that leave the hospital?"

Kennedy was knocking on the door and coming on in at the same time.

Kennedy: Hey, hey, hey, what's going on, guys? I could hear you both from the hallway.

Dr. Baker and Jackson just stared at each other.

On the next episode, Jackson reveals a shocking secret to Dr. Baker and Kennedy.

Episode 9

Diane was sitting in waiting room with Ivan waiting for Dr. Baker to come. Diane hadn't left the hospital once since she got the news about Mystery. Even though she was exhausted, she was not about to leave the hospital until she knew Mystery was going to be ok. She looked over at Ivan.

Diane: You okay, baby?

Ivan: I'm hungry.

Diane: We will go get something in a few minutes okay.

Ivan: Okay. Grandma?

Diane: Yes, baby.

Ivan: Have my dad found my mom?

Diane: (Confused.) What do you mean, Ivan?

Ivan: We don't know where she is.

Diane didn't know what to think by what she was hearing. "Ivan, when was the last time you seen your mom?"

Ivan: I don't know. It's been a long time.

Diane needed to smooth this over with Ivan and get to the bottom of it. "Well, I am sure your dad is going to find her." Diane then gave Ivan a hug. She reached in her purse and got her cell to call Brazil. It went straight to voice mail. Not only did she wanted to find out what was going on with Ivy but she needed to tell him not to go see Mystery. She continued to wait with Ivan. Diane didn't noticed but the mystery person was watching her the whole time.

MYSTERY'S ROOM

Mystery was sitting up in the bed when there was a knock on the door.

Mystery: Come in.

It was Clay.

Mystery: Clay, what's up, buddy? How you been?

Clay went on in. "I've been good. Looks like you have gotten yourself all hurt up."

Mystery: Yeah it seems that way. I can't remember what happen but your dad told me I fell from a fourth-floor balcony. How in the world I manage to do that is beyond me. So what's been going on with you? I haven't seen you in a minute.

Clay: Just school, that's about it.

Mystery: Going to be the next doctor like your dad, huh?

Mystery noticed that Clay didn't seem to be too happy. "Clay, is everything okay? You seem upset."

Clay, teary-eyed, said, "I'm just worried about you, that's all."

Mystery: Aww, buddy, I'm going to be okay. I will be out of here in no time. I bet Malik and Mason are worried like crazy too. I love those guys. Have you seen them?

Clay: No, I haven't.

Mystery: I'm so thirsty.

Clay: You want me to go get you something?

Mystery: Will you please?

Clay: Sure, I will be right back.

DOWNTOWN CAFÉ

Sarah hadn't seen or hung out with her brother Caleb since he'd been out of prison. They were really close and Sarah was very upset when he had to go away. She decided to take him out to lunch so they could catch up.

Caleb: Thanks, sis.

Sarah: For what?

Caleb: For getting me out that house.

Sarah laughed. "It can't be that bad. It's got to be better than prison."

Caleb: Well, that's true. Mom and Dad just be hovering over me so much.

Sarah: Come on, Caleb. They missed you. We all do.

Caleb: Yeah, I guess. So what's been going on with you? How's life been treating you?

Sarah: I definitely can't complain. I have a good job that I love and my own place.

Caleb: No boyfriend.

Sarah: Nooooo. I don't have the time.

Caleb: Don't let time pass you by. We are not getting any younger. You should enjoy your life while you can.

Sarah: And where is all this coming from?

Caleb: I'm just saying. I do want to ask you a question though.

Sarah: What is it?

Caleb: Sarah, have you seen Ana?

DR. BAKER'S OFFICE

Kennedy: Well, is someone going to tell me what's going on? Why are you two arguing?

Dr. Baker: (Crossing his arms.) Ask him.

Kennedy looked at Jackson.

Kennedy: Jackson, what's going on?

Trying to change the subject, Jackson said, "Nothing. What are you doing here?"

Kennedy: Joshua called me but that's not what I asked. Why are you two arguing?

Dr. Baker: I will tell you. Mr. "Help a Stranger" here help Mason leave the hospital yesterday.

Kennedy: What. How do you even know this kid?

Dr. Baker: That's the million-dollar question I've been asking.

Kennedy: Jackson, you do know if Clay press charges for what Mason did to him, he will be going to jail.

Dr. Baker blurted out, "And he will be pressing charges. I will be making sure of that."

Jackson: I bet you will. Look I didn't know what Mason did when I came and got him. He just made it seem that it was an urgency that he leave the hospital, almost like a life-and-death situation.

Kennedy: Jackson, this kid is trouble. I have to agree with Joshua on this one. How could you just help a random stranger?

Jackson was boiling at this point. He yelled, "He is not a stranger, okay. He is not some random kid."

Kennedy and Dr. Baker were surprised at how Jackson was responding.

Kennedy: What a minute. Something is not right with this situation. Jackson, what is it that you're not telling us?

Jackson: Forget it.

Dr. Baker: You see what I mean. I thought we were all best friends here. I see I was wrong. Best friends don't keep secrets from each other. Then you say you love our kids like they're your own. That's a bunch a crap.

Jackson: How can you say that to me?

Dr. Baker: Be a friend to Mason.

Jackson: (Raising his voice again.) He is not my friend!

Dr. Baker: (Raising his voice back at Jackson.) Then what the hell is he to you!

Jackson: HE'S MY SON!

On the next episode, Sarah gives Caleb shocking news.

Episode 10

Alexandria was finally released from the hospital and glad to be home. Brazil made sure she had everything she needed.

Alexandria: I am so glad to be home.

Brazil: Do you need anything? Water? Something to eat?

Alexandria: No, I'm okay. I'm glad you are here with me.

Brazil smiled and said, "You are stuck with me for life. I am going to make sure both you and the baby have no worries. I'm going to be the best father."

Alexandria: I know you are.

There was a knock at the door.

Alexandria: Who could that be?

Brazil: I don't know, but I will get it.

Brazil went to answer the door. It was Adriana, Max, and Jase.

Brazil, not knowing who they were, said, "May I help you?"

Adriana: I'm Adriana, Alexandria's sister.

Brazil: Oh, I'm sorry. Come on in. I'm Brazil.

Adriana and Max shook his hands. Adriana and Jase rushed on over to Alexandria and gave her hug.

Adriana: I am so glad to see you are doing better. Looking better to.

Jase: I was worried about you, Mom.

Alexandria: Aww, well, I am all better now and you know what? I know I missed your birthday but I am going to make it up to you, okay?

Jase: Okay.

Brazil: Excuse me. Alexandria, I am going to go back to the hospital to check on Mystery and to pick up my son. You need anything while I'm out?

Alexandria: Oh no, go ahead. Tell him I said hello.

Brazil: Okay, I will.

Brazil gave her a kiss and left.

DR. BAKER'S OFFICE

Dr. Baker and Kennedy both could not believe what they just heard.

Dr. Baker: What did you just say?

Jackson: Mason is my son.

Dr. Baker: Don't jerk me around right now, Jackson. I am not in the mood for one of your pranks.

Kennedy: I agree.

Jackson: I'm not joking. It's true. Mason is my son.

Kennedy: How? I mean I know how but you never told us you had a son.

Jackson: No one knew but me, Mason, and Mason's mother.

Kennedy: Why would you keep something like that from us? We are your best friends.

Jackson: I know. I just didn't need my best friends judging me for walking away from my family and my responsibilities. I left Mason and his mother when Mason was a little boy. You both know how I was back then. I didn't want any kids or to be tied down. I liked partying and having the different women. Do I regret what I did? Then I didn't, but I do now because I see how it have impacted Mason's life.

Kennedy: What do you mean?

Jackson: Mason's mom became an alcoholic after I left so it forced him to become a man at an early age doing all sort of things to take care of himself and his mother. Eventually his mom died and he came to me for help. He begged me to take him in because he didn't want to go to foster care. You know what I did? I told him no. I told him I didn't have the time to take care of and look after a little boy, and I literally closed the door in his face. I never heard from him again until out of the blue he called me yesterday needing my help again. After what I did to him, turning him away when he was only a child, I couldn't say no this time. Maybe I should have asked him what happened but I didn't. I didn't know this until he told me but he ran away to keep from going into foster care and lived on the streets. Over the years he watched me. Watch me as I lived this lavish life bringing home different women with no care in the world. That did something to him. He's filled with so much anger and hate. So if you want to blame someone Joshua, blame me for creating a monster but that monster is still my son.

Dr. Baker: No, I don't blame you. I understand now why you did what you did but Mason needs professional help. Where is he?

Jackson: He's at my place for now.

Dr. Baker: You have to get him back to the hospital. With his conditions and without the proper medications, Mason can seriously damage himself for life.

Jackson: I understand. I will get him back to the hospital. I'm sorry about all this.

Dr. Baker: I'm sorry to for going off on you like I did. You're my best friend and I love you, man.

Jackson: (Smiling.) I love you too, brother.

They both hugged it out.

Dr. Baker: Now I need to do my rounds. Can you both meet me back here in a few hours? I have something else to discuss with you.

Kennedy: Sure. I need to run by the house for a minute but I will be back.

Jackson: I will go check on Mason and bring him back.

Dr. Baker: Okay, great. I will talk to you both soon. They all left.

Downtown Café

Sarah: Mom and Dad warned me that you may ask about her.

Caleb: Well, they were right. They told me they haven't seen or heard from her since my trial. That was five years ago.

Sarah: That sounds about right.

Caleb. Sarah, I know if anyone would have heard from her after that it would be you. You and Ana were good friends when we were together.

Sarah: I know.

Caleb: Please, sis, just tell me if you heard from her.

Sarah didn't want to lie to her brother. She loved him and they had a special bond before he left. "Yes, Caleb, I talked to her."

Caleb: (Excited.) You did? How is she? Where is she?

Sarah: Hold on, Caleb. I don't know where she is. I haven't talked to her but once. She called me out of the blue like seven months after the trial.

Caleb: Seven months?

Sarah: Yes.

Caleb: Why she waited so long after to reach out to you?

Sarah: She called me from the hospital.

Caleb: The hospital? Why was she calling from there?

Sarah: (Taking a deep breath.) Mom and Dad are going to kill me for telling you this but you do have a right to know.

Caleb: A right to know what?

Sarah: Ana had a baby. Your baby, Caleb.

Caleb: (Shocked.) What?

On the next episode, Alexandria and Adriana have a heart to heart.

Episode 11

Adriana: Brazil seems to really like you.

Alexandria: Yeah, and I like him too. Jase, can you go play in your room while I talk to Aunt Adriana?

Jase: Okay.

Max: Come on, buddy. Let's go see what kind of games you have back here.

Max and Jase went to the bedroom.

Alexandria: It didn't dawn on me until after you all left the hospital. I know why you had to go back to Florida.

Adriana: Yeah, I never miss his birthday. He and Jase would have been the same age.

Alexandria: Yep. That was something back then though. You and I giving birth a day apart in the same hospital.

Adriana: I know right. Momma would have sworn we planned that.

They both laughed.

Adriana: Then you and Armon took your son and moved to New York while I buried mine.

Adriana getting choked up.

Alexandria: Sis.

Adriana: It's okay. I'm fine. CJ is in a much better place now. Anyway enough of all that. What did the doctor say about you and the baby?

Alexandria: We are both healthy. I just need to rest and avoid stress.

Adriana: That means Armon.

Alexandria: I can't avoid him. He is Jase's father and will always be in my life.

Adriana: Yes, but you are going to have to not let him stress you out when he is around.

Alexandria: You are right.

Adriana: Okay, Max and I are going to go get check in but we will be back. Are you going to be okay here alone?

Alexandria: Yea, I will be fine. Brazil will be back soon.

Adriana: Okay. Max?

Max came from the back. "Alexandria, the trip must have tired Jase out. He fell asleep on me."

Alexandria: Oh, okay.

Adriana: You ready to go?

Max: Yep.

Alexandria walked them out.

DOWNTOWN CAFÉ

Caleb: A baby?

Sarah: Yes.

Caleb began to tear up and laugh at the same time. "I have a baby. I'm a father."

Sarah: (Smiling.) Yes.

Caleb: I need to find her. Do you have any clue where she could be?

Sarah: I don't. I'm sorry. The only reason she called me was to let me know about the baby and to tell me she was leaving town for good. She begged me not to tell Mom and Dad about the baby. She wanted to raise him own her own away from here.

Caleb: Him?

Sarah: Yes, she had a baby boy.

Caleb sat back in the chair. "I have a son?"

Sarah: Yes.

Caleb: Mom and Dad knew and didn't tell me.

Sarah: They probably didn't want you to know right now. They want you to get yourself together first.

Caleb: Sarah, I have a son. This changes everything. I have to find Ana. I have to see my son. Let's go. Take me home.

Caleb stood up. Sarah had no other choice but to leave. She began to wonder was it a good idea to have told him this.

On the next episode, Mystery learns the truth.

Episode 12

Sarah drove Caleb back home. As soon as she pulled in the driveway and before she could switch the car off, Caleb was opening the door and rushing out. She switched off and hurried behind him. Caleb rushed in the house.

Caleb: Mom? Dad? Where are you?

Rebecca: In the kitchen.

Caleb and Sarah headed in the kitchen. Rebecca and Kennedy both were in there. Caleb overly excited said, "Why you didn't tell me Ana had a baby."

To both of Kennedy and Rebecca surprised, they both looked at Sarah.

Rebecca: Sarah.

Caleb: Don't blame Sarah. Why didn't either one of you tell me?

Kennedy: We were going to tell you. We just wanted you to focus on yourself first. You haven't been out of prison long, son.

Caleb: I know, Dad, but this changes everything. I definitely have to find her now. I have to see my son. Don't you want to see your grandson?

Kennedy: Of course we would like that but we don't know where Ana is.

Caleb: Dad, you are the chief of police. You can search for her. Put out one of those look out things for her.

Kennedy: Caleb, it's not that simple.

Caleb: (Angry now.) Why you don't want to help me? I just want to find my child.

Everyone was silent now. Caleb was looking at everyone's face. He realized that he wasn't going to get the help from his family.

Caleb: You know what? Don't worry about it. I will get the help and find her myself.

Caleb stormed out of the kitchen and out of the house.

Sarah: Don't worry I will go get him.

Rebecca: Kennedy, do you think we should have told him about the baby sooner?

Kennedy: No, but it's too late now.

Rebecca: I think you should help him now that he knows the truth. That way, when you do find her, you can be there when they come face-to-face to prevent anything wrong from happening.

Kennedy: I think you're right. When Sarah brings him back, I will let him know. He definitely don't need to be on street right now with this rage in him.

At the Hospital

Mystery was half asleep when there was a knock on his door.

Mystery: Come in.

Brazil walked in. "Hey, bro."

Mystery thought he was asleep. He sat up in the bed. He couldn't believe what he was seeing.

Brazil: Damn, Mystery, you look like you've seen a ghost.

Mystery: Who are you?

Brazil: (Laughing.) Good one, man, pretending you don't know who I am. Humor is a good thing. How are you feeling?

Mystery: (Confused.) Okay, I guess. Look, I honestly don't know who you are.

Brazil saw that Mystery was not joking.

Brazil: You're serious? You really don't remember me?

Mystery: (Agitated.) No, no I don't and it's beginning to get frustrating. I don't even know why I am here.

Brazil: I'm your twin brother.

Brazil began to fill Mystery in on everything, not knowing that he weren't supposed to.

Mystery heart monitor started to increase. Brazil didn't notice.

Mystery: What do you mean we are brothers and this Diane person is our mother?

Mystery started to become more agitated. "Where is my mom? I want to see Gloria?"

Brazil: Mystery, what are you saying? Gloria died a while ago.

Mystery: (Breathing heavily.) What?

Brazil: (Confused.) Wait a minute, you don't remember that either?

Mystery continued to breathe heavily. "What? My mom is dead?" Mystery started to grasp for air.

Brazil: Calm down, Mystery.

Mystery's eyes went to the back of his head and his body started shaking uncontrollably. Brazil yelled out, "HELP, HELP!"

On the season finale, Adriana comes face-to-face with her past.

Episode 13

Caleb was walking down the street when a car pulled up beside him. It was Sarah.

Sarah: Caleb?

Caleb kept walking. Sarah switched off and jumped out to go catch up to him. When she did she grabbed his arm.

Sarah: Caleb, where are you going?

Caleb: Why? Does it matter?

Sarah: Of course it matters. Come on, Caleb, this is me. Talk to me.

Caleb: There is nothing to talk about. My main focus right now is trying to find Ana and my son.

Sarah: I understand that. That's why I am going to help you.

Caleb: (Surprised.) Seriously?

Sarah: Yes. I have some friends at the law firm I work for who know people in high places. I can see what I can find out for you.

Caleb hugged his sister. "Thank you so much, sis. I love you."

Sarah: You have to stay cool though. This will not happen overnight.

Caleb: I know. You are right.

Sarah: Now can we get in the car now and leave.

Caleb: (Smiling.) Sure. I need you to take me by the store anyways. I need some cigarettes to calm my nerves.

They both got in the car and left.

JACKSON'S CONDO

Jackson had made it home. He knew it was going to be a fight trying to get Mason to go back to the hospital. He was willing to do whatever it took to get him back there, even calling the police if he had to. Jackson went inside. He yelled out, "Mason?" There was no answer. He called out again, "Mason?" Still no answer.

Jackson walked back to the guest bedroom Mason was sleeping in. He knocked. "Mason, are you sleep?" No answer. Jackson went into the room. No Mason. He saw a note on the bed address to him. As soon as he opened the note $500 fell out. "What's this?" Jackson picked up the money and read the note. The note read, "Sorry to be an inconvenience for the second time in your life. Here is $500 for your troubles."

Jackson sat on the bed and took a deep breath and said, "Mason, where are you, son?"

MALIK'S HOUSE

Malena had been worried about Armon since he stormed out on her. She had been trying to reach him on his cell but couldn't. She decided to call again. It went straight to the voice mail.

Malena: Armon, this is Malena. Call me. I am worried about you.

Malena hung up. Then she decided to call Malik.

The cell phone rang.

Malik: Hello?

Malena: Hey, baby. Are you okay out there?

Malik: Hey, yeah, I'm okay. I'm pulling up to this abandon farm-house right now. We got an anonymous call that there was a car in a lake behind the house.

Malena: Oh.

Malik: Yeah, so let me call you back. The workers are already here fixing to pull the car out of the water.

Malena: Okay, be careful. I love you.

Malik: Love you too.

They hung up. Malik walked up to the crew. "What we got fellows?"

Crewman: Pulling the vehicle out now.

As the machine pulled the car out of the water, Malik started walking closer. His eyes getting bigger in disbelief. The machine finally got the car completely out the water.

Malik: Oh my God.

Crewman: What is it, sir? Do you know who car this is?

Malik: Yes, it's my sister's.

AT THE HOSPITAL

Brazil ran out of the room. When he did he ran right into Dr. Baker. Diane was walking down the hall with Ivan at the same time and saw him.

Dr. Baker: Brazil, you're not supposed to be in there.

Brazil: (Scared.) Please, Doctor, something is happening to him.

Dr. Baker yelled out, "Nurse I need you," as they ran back into the room.

Dr. Baker: He's seizing. Nurse, put something between his teeth.

Diane picked up Ivan and ran to the room as well. "What's happening?"

Dr. Baker: (Addressing both Diane and Brazil.) I need you both out right now!

Nurse: (Yelling.) He's crashing.

Dr. Baker: Give me the defibrillator.

Diane: What's happening to my son?

Another nurse ran into the room. She escorted Diane and Brazil out. She closed the door as they watched Dr. Baker work on Mystery.

Diane: (Crying.) Brazil, what happened in there?

Brazil: I don't know. Everything happened so fast.

Brazil and Diane continued to wait. About fifteen minute later Dr. Baker came out. Diane watched him as he took his cap off and shook his head.

Diane: (Screaming.) Noooooooo!

AT THE STORE

Max and Adriana were heading to the hotel when he noticed he needed to get gas.

Max: I need to stop here and get some gas.

Adriana: Okay. I will go in and get some drinks for later.

They both got out. Max started pumping the gas while Adriana went inside. She had picked up some snacks and drinks when she heard the bell ring. Someone else was coming in the store. She headed for the counter but had to wait for the customer in front of her getting cigarettes. The customer asked the store clerk how much for the cigarettes? Adriana looked up. She recognized that voice. The customer asked the store clerk for a lighter as well. Adriana knew that voice. She dropped everything she had to floor. The sound of everything hitting the floor caught the store clerk and customer's attention. The customer turned around. Adriana froze in place. She couldn't believe her eyes.

Adriana: Caleb?

Caleb: (Shocked.) Ana?

ALEXANDRIA'S HOUSE

Alexandria was lying across her bed resting when she heard this loud banging on her door.

Alexandria: Oh my God, who is knocking on my door like this?

She got up to go answer. Another loud knock came. "I'm coming," she yelled.

Alexandria, not thinking to look out the peephole, snatched the door open. "Yes?"

It was Armon. He was drunk and Alexandria could tell.

Alexandria: Armon, what are you doing here?

Armon: Why didn't you let me know they released you from the hospital? I am still your husband.

Alexandria: Armon, what do you want?

Armon: You could let me in. We didn't finish our conversation at the hospital.

Alexandria: Look at you. You're drunk, and I am not fixing to do this with you now.

Alexandria tried to close the door, but Armon, in anger, kicked it open and went on in.

Alexandria: Armon.

Armon: (Yelling.) You're not going to dismiss me.

Alexandria: Keep your voice down. Jase is in his room, sleeping. You need to leave.

Armon: I am not going anywhere until we decide what we are going to do.

Alexandria: Do about what?

Armon: This baby you're carrying.

Alexandria: This baby has nothing to do with you.

Armon, staggering, got in her face. "You are not having this child. You are my wife."

Alexandria: We are not together and will never be again. This is my child, and I am having it.

Armon grabbed her by both arms. "You think I'm going to let you make a fool of me like this."

Alexandria, struggling, said, "Let go of me." She broke free then slapped Armon. "Don't your ever put your hands on me again."

Armon stood there for a second, then he slapped her back, knocking her to the floor. Alexandria got up and ran to her bedroom. Armon grabbed her by the hair before she could make it through the bedroom door. "You are not having this baby." He shoved her to the floor. Alexandria crawled quickly to her bed and reached under it, pulling out her gun she always kept there. She turned around and fired two shots. The first shot missed Armon but the second one grazed his ear. He grabbed his ear.

Armon: You bitch. You shot me.

Alexandria: (Breathing heavily.) Now get out.

All of a sudden, there was a hard thump. Armon turned around. Alexandria looked passed Armon. Her eyes got big, then she screamed. Jase had fallen to the floor. The first bullet that missed Armon hit Jase in the chest. She got up and ran to him, screaming. Armon was dazed at what he was seeing, his son laying there with blood pouring out of his chest.

To be continued.

PART 6

Episode 1

Melanie and her boyfriend Chris have been seeing each other for over six months now. Although she was fourteen and he was seventeen, she knew her parents would not allow it. When they weren't seeing each other at school, they would have to sneak out at night and meet up. Being that they live so close together, she would even sneak over to his house sometimes, but he had never been to hers. It was getting late, and she knew her mom would be going to bed soon. She decided to call Chris.

The phone rang.

Chris: Hello.

Melanie: Hey. What you doing?

Chris: Just sitting here watching TV. What about you?

Melanie: Just lying here, thinking about you.

Chris: Aww, babe. I'm always thinking about you.

Melanie: I have an idea.

Chris: What's that?

Melanie: I want to see. How about you come over to my house tonight?

Chris: Are you serious? That's too risky. You already told me your bedroom is right next to your parents.

Melanie: I know that. Just hear me out. We can meet in our basement. It's a lot of space and even a bathroom down there. You can come in like an hour. I know my mom and sister will be sleep by then.

Chris: (Nervous.) I don't know about that.

Melanie: Don't you want to see me?

Chris: Of course I do, but what if we get caught?

Melanie: We won't. My dad is working until in the morning. My mom and sister will be sleeping. Look, you are coming and that's that.

Chris: Okay, but I will be uncomfortable.

Melanie: I have something to make you comfortable.

They both started laughing.

Melanie: You need to come to the side of the house. We have an outside door that leads down into the basement. We keep the door padlocked from the inside so be there in an hour, and I will unlock it for you.

Chris: Okay, I will be there. Love you.

Melanie: Love you too.

They both hung up.

AT THE POLICE STATION

Malik was sitting at his desk, thinking about Ivy. There were still no leads. When they pulled Ivy's car from the lake, Malik ordered forensics to go through the entire car. He was hoping they could find something that may lead them to her. Another officer walked up.

Police officer: Here is the forensic report you asked for.

The police officer handed Malik the folder. Malik quickly opened it and started reading it. He saw that nothing was found. Frustrated, Malik threw the report across his desk. He was back to square one.

Malik: Where are you, sis?

AT THE STORE

Caleb: (Surprised.) Ana?

Caleb couldn't believe it was her. "Ana." He went to reach for her but she backed away, then she ran out of the store. Caleb took off behind her.

Store Clerk: (Yelled out.) Hey you forgot your cigarettes.

Sarah was sitting in the car texting when she noticed a woman run by the car, frantic. She didn't realize it was Adriana. Then she saw Caleb run by after the woman. Sarah jumped out the car. "Caleb?"

Max has just finished pumping the gas. As he was walking around the car, he saw a man chasing Adriana.

Adriana: (Yelling.) Max! Max!

Max ran to her. Adriana ran into his arms, nervous and hysterical. Caleb ran up.

Max: Why the hell are you chasing my wife?

Caleb: I'm sorry. Ana, look at me. I'm not going to hurt you.

Ana had her face buried in Max's chest and holding on tight.

Max: I suggest you back off right now.

Sarah ran up. "Caleb, what's going on?"

Caleb: (Pointing at Adriana.) Look, its Ana.

Sarah: What? Ana, is that you?

Max: Her name is Adriana.

Sarah: Oh my God, it is you.

Caleb: Ana, can I talk to you for a minute?

Adriana: Max, please get me out of here.

Sarah: No, wait. Caleb is leaving Ana.

Caleb: What? No, I am not.

Sarah pulled Caleb to the side. "Look, Caleb, you need to let me handle this. Look at her, she is not fixing to talk to you right now. Now she may talk to me, but you need to go back to the car if you want to have any chance of finding out about your son.

Caleb understood. He walked back to the car. Sarah went back to Adriana who was still holding on to Max.

Sarah: Ana, Caleb is gone. I sent him back to the car. Now can you turn around and let me see you. It's been so long.

Adriana turned around very slowly.

Sarah: (Smiled.) Look at you.

Adriana: Sarah?

Sarah nodded her head with tears in her eyes. Adriana walked up to her and gave her a hug.

Sarah: Oh, I missed you so much.

Adriana: I've missed you to.

Sarah: Ana, I know this is not the time or the place, but I want to catch up and talk to you.

Adriana: You're right. This is not the place. We are staying at the Westin downtown. Meet me in the lobby in an hour. Please, Sarah, do not tell Caleb or bring him. I'm not ready for that yet.

Sarah: I promise it will be only me.

Max: Come on, babe. Let's go.

They got in the car and left.

Sarah went back to the car where Caleb was standing outside, waiting.

Caleb: (Impatient.) Well, tell me. What did she say?

Sarah: She doesn't want to see you right now, but she will see me.

Caleb: Sarah, I need to talk to her.

Sarah: I understand that, but that is not going to happen right now. You need to let me talk for you. Her emotions are all over the place right now rightfully so. Trust me, I will find out all you want to know. Please, Caleb, this is a delicate situation and you need to let me handle it for now. We don't want her leaving town again, do we?

Caleb: No.

Sarah: So are you going to let me handle it?

Caleb: Yes.

Sarah: Good. She told to me to come see her in an hour so I'm going to take you home and head over to where she is staying and no I can't tell you where.

Caleb: I understand.

They both left the store.

ALEXANDRIA'S HOUSE

Alexandria was screaming and crying hysterically. She had mistakenly shot her own son.

Alexandria: NO! NO! WHAT HAVE I DONE!

Armon snapped out of his trance. He knew he had to do something to save his son. He kneeled down beside Jase.

Alexandria pushed him away yelling, "GET AWAY FROM HIM! GET AWAY!"

Armon grabbed her hands. "Listen to me. You can hate me later. Right now, we need to worry about Jase. You know I am an ex-policeman so I am somewhat trained in this type of situation. We need to turn him over to see if the bullet went straight through."

Alexandria listened. They turned Jase over and saw there was no exit wound.

Armon: Okay, the bullet is still in his chest.

Alexandria: I'm fixing to call the ambulance.

Armon: The ambulance is going to take forever. My boy is not going to die today.

Armon picked Jase up.

Alexandria: What are you doing?

Armon: I'm not waiting for the ambulance. We are going to take him ourselves. Go get a towel. We need to keep pressure on this wound.

Alexandria ran to the bathroom and got a towel. She came back and gave it to Armon. Armon pressed it hard on the wound.

Armon: Let's go. You can call the doctor from the car.

They both ran out of the house with Jase.

KENNEDY'S HOUSE

Sarah pulled into the driveway to let Caleb out.

Sarah: Let Mom and Dad know what happened. I'm going to head over to see Ana.

Caleb: Sarah, you have to find out about my son. How he's doing? Everything.

Sarah: I will find out everything for you. Trust me, okay?

Caleb: I do, sis.

Caleb got out the car and watched as Sarah pulled off. He ran into the house.

Caleb: Mom? Dad? Where are you?

Rebecca: We're in the living room.

Caleb ran into the living room all excited.

Rebecca: What's going on?

Caleb couldn't do anything but go to laughing. He went and kissed his mom on the cheek. Then he went over and gave his dad a big hug.

Kennedy: What's gotten into you?

Caleb: This has turned out to be one of the best days of my life.

Kennedy: Really now? That's not how you acted when you left out of here earlier.

Caleb: I know. I'm sorry about that but I have some wonderful news.

Rebecca: What is it, baby?

Caleb: I saw Ana today.

Kennedy: You what?

On the next episode, Kennedy and Rebecca learns that Ana is in town.

Episode 2

An hour had passed. Melanie got up and went to look in on her mom and sister. They both were fast asleep. She grabbed a blanket, pillow, and a candles from her bedroom and headed downstairs quietly. When she got the kitchen, she lit the candle from the stove. She didn't want to use the basement lights just in case someone came to the kitchen and saw it. She headed on down to the basement. She sat the candle on the floor and laid out the blanket and pillow. She picked up the candle and looked around for the padlock keys. She knew her parents always left them out. Then she spotted them. The keys were in the lock on the storage room door where Ivy was being kept. Melanie didn't know Ivy was in there. Ivy was taped up and had fallen asleep so she didn't hear anything. Melanie didn't want to make too much noise with the keys so she gently slid them out the lock. She headed to the stairs that led to the outside. She unlocked the padlock and opened the door. Chris was standing there.

At the Hospital

Diane: (Crying uncontrollably.) No, not my son.

Dr. Baker: (Taking her by the arms.) He's going to be okay.

Brazil: Doc, are you sure?

Dr. Baker: Yes, I'm sure. He is going to be fine.

Diane: The impression you gave when you came out the room.

Dr. Baker cut her off. "I'm sorry for that. I'm going to honest with you though. Mystery did flatline in there, but I worked to bring him back. I'm sorry for the impression I gave but he just gave me a scare.

Diane: Can we see him?

Dr. Baker: I'm afraid not. During the seizure he was having, his blood pressure went through the roof. The information you gave him Brazil was too much for him to handle.

Brazil: I didn't know.

Diane: I've been calling you to tell you not to go see him. Mystery has lost the last five years of his memory.

Brazil: That's why he was acting like he didn't know me. Damn, what have I done?

Dr. Baker: It's okay now. I have him sedated so he should sleep for a while. The nurse is going to come get him in a few minutes and run some tests for me.

Dr. Baker: (Addressing Diane.) Diane, can I talk to you alone for a second. This is more personal.

Diane looked at Brazil.

Brazil: Oh, go ahead. I'm going to run home for a few minutes. I need to change clothes and get something to eat. I will take Ivan with me. Call me if there is any change with Mystery.

Diane: Okay, son, I will.

Brazil left with Ivan. Diane turned to Dr. Baker.

Diane: What do you need to talk about?

Dr. Baker: I just wanted you to know that Kennedy and Jackson are meeting me in my office in a little bit. I'm going to talk and tell them about you, Brazil, and Mystery.

Diane: I want to be there when you talk to them.

Dr. Baker: Diane, I don't think that's a good idea.

Diane: Joshua, I need to be there.

Dr. Baker: Okay, we don't know what kind of reaction we will get from them. I just want you to be prepared.

Diane: I can handle it.

Dr. Baker: Okay then, let's go.

They both walked back to his office.

KENNEDY'S HOUSE

Rebecca: Did you say you saw Ana?

Caleb: Yes, Mom, I did.

Kennedy: Caleb, stop joking around. Are you serious?

Caleb: Yes, Dad. I wouldn't joke about this. Sarah saw her too.

Kennedy and Rebecca saw that he was serious now.

Rebecca: How?

Caleb: We ran into her at the store surprisingly.

Kennedy: Son, you didn't do anything crazy, did you?

Caleb: Just tried to talk to her, but she didn't want to talk to me. She did talk and agree to see Sarah. That's where Sarah is gone now, to see her.

Kennedy: Wow, what are the odds of that after all this time.

Caleb: Dad, I need your help. Can you find out where she is staying and at least have a cop keeping track of her until we find out about my son.

Kennedy: Son, now that I will do. I was just about to head out to the hospital to go see your Uncle Joshua. I will go by the station when I leave there.

Caleb: Thanks, Dad.

Caleb gave his dad a hug. Kennedy kissed Rebecca and left.

At the Hospital

Armon and Alexandria had made it the hospital with Jase. She had already called Dr. Walker from the car. She had tried calling Adriana but couldn't get an answer so she called and spoke with Max letting him know what had happened. Armon and Alexandria ran into the hospital. Armon was carrying Jase. Dr. Walker was waiting at the nurse's station. When he saw them running into the hospital, he met them with a stretcher.

Dr. Walker: Here, lay him on here.

Armon: Doc, there's no exit wound.

Dr. Walker felt his neck for a pulse.

Dr. Walker: His pulse is very week. We got to get him into surgery right now.

Alexandria: Dr. Walker, is he going to be okay?

Dr. Walker: I am going to do everything I can, okay? It looks like Jase has lost a lot of blood. The best thing you both can do right now is go with the nurse and give some blood. Jase will need it. Now I need to go.

Dr. Walker rolled Jase away. Alexandria was still crying. Armon was covered in Jase's blood and just watched as Dr. Walker took him away.

Nurse: I need you both to come with me.

Armon and Alexandria left with the nurse.

On the next episode, Adriana and Sarah meet.

Episode 3

Chris: What took you so long to open the door?

Melanie: I had to find the keys. It's dark down here, and I only have this candle.

Chris: Why don't you cut on some lights?

Melanie: No. Are you crazy? If anyone comes down to the kitchen, they will see the basement lights on crazy.

Chris: Oh, okay.

Melanie took Chris hands and pulled him close to her. They gave each other a long, passionate kiss.

Melanie: Happy to see me?

Chris: Always.

They kissed again. Then Melanie led him over to the pad she made on the floor. Chris looked around.

"What's in there?" he said, pointing at the storage room.

Melanie: Nothing just a lot of old clothes and dusty boxes. Come on, let's lay on the pad.

They both laid down. Melanie laid in his arms. Melanie was fourteen and was still a virgin. Chris knew that and never forced or pressured her about. They started kissing again.

Melanie: I love you.

Chris: I love you too. How long can we stay down here?

Melanie: We can sleep down here for a few hours. Then I will need to go back upstairs.

Chris: Cool.

They both laid there and fell asleep in each other arms.

At the Hotel

Sarah was in the hotel lobby, waiting for Adriana. They both used to be best friends. Sarah had a lot of questions but wasn't going to force anything. Adriana walked up behind her.

Adriana: Hey, Sarah.

Sarah: Ana, hey.

They both hugged.

Sarah: Thanks for letting me come see you. We have so much catching up to do.

Adriana: Did you come alone?

Sarah: Yes, I told you I would and I didn't tell him where you were staying either.

Adriana: Thank you.

Sarah: But, Ana, I think you should hear him out.

Adriana: Are you serious? He raped me.

Sarah: I understand, and I've never condoned that. He deserved everything he got for doing that to you.

Adriana: Caleb and I was dating for almost a year and I trusted him. Even though we were separated, Caleb knew it was always a possibility that me and Max would get back together. He just wasn't hearing that when that time came. He hurt me deeply, Sarah.

Sarah: He feels awful for what he did. He truly regrets it and wanted to tell you face-to-face.

Adriana: I don't know if I am ready for that yet.

Sarah: There is no rush. Take your time, but I wouldn't plead for him if he wasn't sincere. You were my best friend and I wouldn't lie to you either.

Adriana: I will think about it. That's all I can say right now.

Sarah: I understand. Now let's change the subject. The last time we spoke you called me from the hospital saying you had given birth to a baby boy. How is my nephew? Do you have any pictures?

Adriana just lowered her head. Sarah saw her reaction.

Sarah: Ana, is everything okay? Did I say something wrong?

Adriana: No, you didn't say anything wrong. My baby died.

Sarah covered her mouth with both hands. Her eyes begin to fill with tears.

Sarah: Ana, nooooooo. I am so, so sorry.

Adriana: It's okay. I have learned to cope with it over the years.

Max ran up.

Adriana: Max, is everything okay?

Max: No. Alexandria's been calling you.

Adrianna: (Looking at her phone.) Oh, I have it on silent. What's wrong?

Max: We need to get to the hospital. Jase's been hurt.

Adriana: Oh my God.

Sarah: (Standing up.) Go ahead.

Adriana: Jase is my nephew. Leave your number at the front desk for me. I promise I will call.

Sarah: Okay.

Max and Adriana ran out of the hotel.

DR. BAKER'S OFFICE

Dr. Baker and Diane were waiting in his office for Kennedy and Jackson to arrive. Diane was pacing back and forth.

Diane: I'm nervous, Joshua.

Dr. Baker: There is nothing to be nervous about, trust me. For what it's worth, I think you're doing the right thing.

Diane: I don't know.

Dr. Baker: You're not changing your mind, are you?

Diane: No, this whole situation just has me nervous, that's all. I know I need to do this for my sons.

There was a knock at the door.

Dr. Baker: Come in.

Kennedy and Jackson walked in.

Dr. Baker: Hey, guys. You both must have rode together?

Jackson: We pulled up in the parking lot at the same time.

Dr. Baker: Oh, okay. Guys, this is Diane. Diane, you've met Kennedy once before.

Kennedy: Good to see you again.

They both shook hands.

Diane: Likewise.

Dr. Baker: (Pointing at Jackson.) This is Jackson.

Jackson: Nice to meet you.

They both shook hands.

Diane: Thank you.

Dr. Baker: Okay, I know you both are wondering why I needed to talk to you. Diane is here because she is a part of this as well. Diane and I have been dating for a while now. In getting to know each other, we discovered something.

Kennedy: Discovered what?

Dr. Baker: Do you both remember our summer break in college, when we went to New York for the baseball game?

Kennedy: Somewhat yeah.

Jackson: I do. That was a long, long time ago.

Dr. Baker: Twenty-six years. Do you guys remember picking up a young lady on the street one night and taking her back to the hotel?

Jackson: (Smiling.) Now I remember that. She was a hot prostitute.

Diane lowered her head in shame.

Kennedy: Joshua, do you think we should be talking about this in front of Diane?

Dr. Baker: She is aware of everything that happened. Are you okay, Diane?

Diane: Yes, I'm okay.

Dr. Baker: I know you both remembered what took place that night in that room.

Jackson: (Still smiling.) I sure do.

Kennedy: I do, too, but what has this got to do with Diane. I don't think she should be hearing us rehash that night. No offense, Diane, I'm just showing respect.

Diane: Joshua, let me finish telling it.

Dr. Baker: Are you sure?

Diane: Yes. Kennedy, Jackson, I know all about that night.

Kennedy: You couldn't possibly.

Diane: I do because I am the prostitute you picked up that night.

Kennedy: What?

Jackson's smile dropped.

Diane: I am Trixie.

On the next episode, Sarah lies to protect Caleb.

Episode 4

Sarah had made it back from her visit with Adriana. She knew that Caleb was going to be devastated when he heard the news that his baby was dead.

Sarah: Knock, knock, it's me.

Rebecca: I'm in the kitchen.

Sarah went to the kitchen. Before she could say anything, Caleb rushed from the back room.

Caleb: What happened?

Sarah: Calm down. It went okay.

Caleb: Tell me what she said. How is my baby?

Sarah: Caleb, she still doesn't want to see you right now. I did get her to consider it, though. She is going to think about it. You're just going to have to give it some time.

Caleb: What did she say about the baby? She can't keep me away from my son.

Sarah started to think. She had to make a decision on rather to tell him the truth or not. She didn't want to hurt her brother. She definitely didn't want him to do anything crazy and go back to jail. Rebecca was observing her the whole time.

Sarah: She gave the baby up for adoption the day he was born.

Caleb: Why would she do that?

Rebecca: Exactly. She could have just given the baby to me and your father if she didn't want him.

Sarah: I'm sorry, Caleb. She did say we will be talking again. I will make sure I find out more for you. I just didn't want to push her too much on this first visit.

Caleb: Yeah, I understand. I'm going to bed.

Rebecca: Son, you okay?

Caleb just left the kitchen without saying a word.

Sarah: Okay, I guess I will be heading home to. I will come by tomorrow. Love you, Mom.

Sarah started to leave but Rebecca stopped her.

Rebecca: Wait a minute. You're not going anywhere. I want to know what really happened to that baby.

DR. BAKER'S OFFICE

Kennedy and Jackson could not believe what they just heard.

Kennedy: What did you say?

Diane: I am Trixie.

Jackson: (Laughing.) Get out of here.

They both saw that Diane and Dr. Baker were not laughing.

Kennedy: Wait a minute, you're serious?

Diane: Yes.

Dr. Baker: It's true.

Kennedy: How do you know it's true?

Dr. Baker: She told me what happened that night detail by detail. Details that no one else would know but us.

Jackson: I am sorry, but I don't believe this.

Dr. Baker: Jackson, I didn't want to believe it either but it's true.

Kennedy: Why come to us with this now? It happened twenty-six years ago. It's in the past.

Dr. Baker and Diane looked at each other.

Kennedy: What is it? What's that look for?

Dr. Baker went and stood behind Diane for support.

Dr. Baker: Go ahead, Diane. Tell them. It's okay.

Jackson: Tell us what?

Diane: (Nervous.) That was the night I got pregnant. I have twin boys and one of you are their father.

On the next episode, Dr. Baker ask Kennedy and Jackson for a DNA test.

Episode 5

Max and Adriana made it to the hospital. They rushed to the nurse's station.

Adriana: Excuse me, there was a young boy brought in not too long ago. His name is Jase.

Nurse: One second, let me check.

The nurse reviewed the login sheet. Adriana was getting antsy.

Adriana: Anything?

Nurse: Here it is. He will be on the fourth floor. His parents should be in the waiting room up there.

Max: Thank you.

They rushed to the elevators.

Adriana: I have a bad feeling, Max.

Max: Don't, okay. We don't know anything.

Elevator doors opened and they got on. Max hit the fourth-floor button.

Max: Let just wait until we talk to Alexandria.

Elevator doors open, and they quickly rushed to the waiting room. Alexandria and Armon was sitting on opposite ends of each other. Max and Adriana rushed in.

Alexandria and Adriana ran to each other and hugged. They both were crying at this point.

Adriana: What happed to Jase?

Alexandria: He was shot.

Max: What?

Adriana: Oh my God, how did that happen? Who would do such a thing to a child?

Alexandria: (Crying.) I did. I shot my baby.

Adriana: You did what?

Kennedy's House

Rebecca: I want to know what really happened to that baby.

Sarah: Mom, I told you.

Rebecca: Girl, who do you think you're talking to. I'm your mama and I can tell when you're lying. Now you may have gotten Caleb to believe that story about the baby being adopted but I didn't.

Sarah: It's the truth. That's what Ana told me.

Rebecca: Sarah, if you lie to me one more time. Now you tell me what happened.

Sarah took a deep breath.

Sarah: Okay, but you can't tell Caleb.

Rebecca: What is it, girl?

Sarah: Ana's baby died.

Rebecca covered her mouth in shock. She pulled out a chair and sat down.

Sarah: Now you see why I lied to Caleb.

Rebecca: Yes, you did right to lie to him. I don't think he can handle that news right now. That poor, poor girl. She has been through so much hurt and turmoil.

Sarah: I know, but I think she eventually will see Caleb. She is thinking about it. Well, I got to go. I will talk to you tomorrow, okay?

Rebecca: Okay.

Sarah gave her a kiss then left. Rebecca stayed sitting at the kitchen table.

Dr. Baker's Office

Jackson and Kennedy just stood there and stared at Diane. They both were speechless by what she just told them.

Dr. Baker: Guys, did you hear what she said?

Kennedy still staring at Diane said calmly, "We heard her." He then looked at Dr. Baker and said, "I'm sorry, but I don't believe it. Kind of far-fetched, don't you think, Josh?"

Dr. Baker: It's a possibility, though.

Jackson began to speak not taking his eyes off Diane.

Jackson: Let me get this straight. You want us to believe that you're the long-lost hooker.

"Jackson," Dr. Baker said, interrupting Jackson but Jackson continued.

Jackson: That we gangbang twenty something years ago.

Dr. Baker: (Angry.) Jackson, enough!

Jackson: No, it's not enough, Joshua. She wants us to believe this and to make even better she has twin sons that may be either mines or Kennedys.

Diane: It's the truth.

Jackson: Lady, what are you looking for? What are you looking to gain?

Diane: (Angry.) Excuse me?

Jackson: Is it money that you want?

Diane: How dare you.

Dr. Baker, stepping in front of Jackson, said, "Jackson, that's enough."

Diane grabbed Dr. Baker by the arm. "It's okay."

Dr. Baker: Are you sure?

Diane: Yes, I will let you finish here. I'll be in the waiting room.

Dr. Baker: Diane, you don't have to leave.

Diane: I know, but it's one thing before I go.

Diane, staring back at Jackson and Kennedy, continued, "My son is in this hospital fighting for his life and you both have the audacity to think I'm playing games right now. Let me tell you both something, I don't want or need either of your monies. Believe that. I am doing this not just for me but for my sons. Looking at things now, my sons are in a lose-lose situation. They either going to have jerk [pointing at Kennedy] or a jackass [pointing at Jackson] for a father." Diane walked out the office.

Dr. Baker: Guys, you didn't have to act like that.

Kennedy: That's easy for you to say. You're not the one being accused.

Dr. Baker: Okay, fair enough. But answer this, you both don't believe her, right?

Kennedy: Absolutely not.

Jackson: Hell, no.

Dr. Baker: Okay, so prove her wrong then.

Kennedy: What do you mean?

Dr. Baker: Do a DNA test.

Jackson: I'm not fixing to go through all that to prove anything.

Kennedy: I'm with Jackson on this one.

Dr. Baker: Okay, guys, just hear me out for a minute. Diane and I have been dating for a while now and I really like her. I think I might even love her. You both know better than anyone how devastated I was when my wife died. I never thought I would feel this way about a woman again but I do. I really see Diane being in my life for a long time. I just don't want this situation to always be hanging over our heads. Look, don't do the test for her. Do it for me. I am asking you both, best friend to best friends. Please take the DNA test for me. I'm begging you both. Kennedy, what you say?

Kennedy: Say please again. I like it when you beg.

Dr. Baker: Please.

Kennedy: Fine then.

Dr. Baker: Jerk.

They both went to laughing.

Dr. Baker: Jackson, what about you.

Jackson: (Taking a deep breath.) Sure, let's just get this done and out the way.

Dr. Baker: Thanks, guys. I owe you one.

Kennedy: Damn right you do. Now what we need to do.

Dr. Baker: Have a seat. I have two DNA kits here. I'm going to have to collect cheek cells from your mouth using a cotton swab. I'm also going to draw some blood to check the blood type as well and that's it.

Dr. Baker withdrew blood from them both and swabbed their mouth.

Jackson: How long will it take for the results?

Dr. Baker: Just a few hours. Good thing is we have a testing lab here in the hospital so we don't have to send the samples off. Also technology has gotten so advanced, we should have the results back in no time. I already have samples from Mystery.

Kennedy: Mystery?

Dr. Baker: Yes, that one of the son's name. The other one is name Brazil. Brazil is Ivan's dad.

Jackson: Wait a minute. Your grandson Ivan?

Dr. Baker: Yep.

Kennedy: Small world.

Dr. Baker: Okay, so I'm going to take these samples downstairs to the test facility. I will call you both just as soon as I get the results so have your phone on.

Kennedy: We will.

They all left Dr. Baker's office.

On the next episode, Alexandria explains what happened to Jase.

Episode 6

Dr. Baker stopped by the nurse's station to get Mystery's chart and test results. He was relieved to see everything was fine. His blood pressure was back down. Clay was sitting in Mystery's room when Dr. Baker walked in.

Clay: Dad.

Dr. Baker: Hey, son. How are you doing?

Clay: I'm fine. Is Mystery going to be okay?

Dr. Baker: Yes, he's going to be fine. He gave me quite a scare at one point.

Clay: The nurse told me what happened. All this is my fault. If I've only been here.

Dr. Baker: Hey, don't do that. Don't beat yourself up about it.

Clay: But I was only gone a minute.

Dr. Baker: Clay, it doesn't matter now. Mystery is going to be okay. The medicine I gave him is going to have him sleeping for a while. Why don't you go home and get some rest yourself?

Clay: No, I'm not leaving him again. I need to be here when he wakes up.

Dr. Baker: You have always been like your mother, stubborn.

Dr. Baker checked Mystery's blood pressure and observed the monitors that were hooked up to him.

Dr. Baker: Okay, I'm done here. I'll be back a little later to check on him. I really wish you would go home and get some rest.

Clay: Dad, I'm fine.

Dr. Baker: Okay, okay suit yourself.

Clay: Have you heard from Ivy?

Dr. Baker: No. I'm going to call your brother when I get back to my office to see have he heard anything.

Clay: Let me know.

Dr. Baker: I will.

Dr. Baker left the room.

WAITING ROOM

Adriana: Alexandria, what do you mean you shot Jase. You wouldn't hurt him for nothing in the world.

Alexandria: I didn't mean to do it.

Adriana: Well, how did it happen?

Armon was listening and watching from the other side of the waiting room.

Adriana: (Looking at Armon.) Wait a minute. Please don't tell me he had something to do with this.

Alexandria didn't say word.

Adriana: I should have known. Alexandria, why were you shooting at him?

Alexandria: He was trying to attack me tonight. He was drunk, and I was so scared for me and the baby. All I could think about was the last time he was drunk and what happened. So I made it to my gun and not thinking I shot at him twice. Jase was supposed to be sleeping. I didn't see him standing there.

Alexandria started to cry. Adriana held her sister. Adriana and Armon just stared at each other with hate in their eyes.

Adriana: It's not your fault. It's too bad you missed.

Armon heard her. He got up and walked out of the waiting room.

Adriana: Have you heard from the doctor yet?

Alexandria: Not yet. He rushed Jase off to surgery.

Adriana: Max, stay with her. I'm going to go see what I can find out.

Max: Okay, babe.

Adriana left the waiting room. Her only intentions were to go find Armon and give him a piece of her mind.

On the next episode, Dr. Baker and Diane confesses their love for each other.

Episode 7

Dr. Baker left Mystery's room heading to the waiting room. He knew Diane would still be there. She was not about to leave the hospital now. He walked in the waiting room. Diane was sitting there reading a magazine.

Dr. Baker: Hey there.

Diane looked up and said, "Hey," with a smile. Dr. Baker went and sat next to her.

Dr. Baker: How are you holding up?

Diane: Okay, I guess.

Dr. Baker: Just want you to know that Mystery's results came back and everything is fine. Blood pressure is back down to normal.

Diane: (Relieved.) Thank God. Is he woke?

Dr. Baker: No. He will be sleeping for a while. Speaking off, when is the last time you rested?

Diane: I don't know. I'm not worried about that.

Dr. Baker: You should be. I want you to go home get some rest. I will call as soon as Mystery wakes up.

Diane: No, not a chance.

Dr. Baker: You should at least go home and shower, eat and put on some fresh clothes.

Diane: (Looking at Dr. Baker funny.) Are you trying to say I stink?

Dr. Baker: (Laughing.) No. I'm just saying. Mystery is not going to be awake for a while. You should at least do these things while he is sleeping.

Diane: Maybe I will. But I am coming right back.

Dr. Baker: Okay. I also want to apologize for my friend's behavior earlier.

Diane: It's okay. I have thick skin.

Dr. Baker: I did get them to take a DNA test though.

Diane was happy. "Are you serious?"

Dr. Baker: It took some arm twisting, but I did.

Diane just hugged Dr. Baker. "Oh, thank you so much, Joshua. You don't know what that mean to me."

Dr. Baker kissed her on top of the head. "No problem at all. I love you."

Dr. Baker surprised himself by saying that. Diane looked at him.

Diane: You love me?

Dr. Baker: I'm sorry, but I do. I told Kennedy and Jackson that I do to. Diane, I haven't felt this way about another woman since my wife. You probably don't feel the same way but . . .

Diane: (Cutting him off.) I do.

Dr. Baker: You do what?

Diane: I love you too. I've loved you for a while now.

That was music to his ears. He gave her a long, passionate kiss.

Dr. Baker: (Laughing.) I love you. I love you.

Diane: (Laughing back.) I love you too.

They continued to kiss. Diane pulled back.

Diane: I better go.

Dr. Baker: Okay.

Diane left the waiting room to go home.

MYSTERY'S ROOM

Clay was sitting there just staring at Mystery. Mystery was still sedated from the medication Dr. Baker had given him. Clay refused to leave his side until he woke up. "I'm not going anywhere you hear me Mystery so you might as well wake up. You're stuck with me now for good." Clay stood up and gave Mystery a kiss on the forehead. Tears filled his eyes. "You wake up for me okay? I promise when you are better, we are going to move away from Atlanta and start over fresh, just you and me." Clay sat back down and just held onto Mystery's hand.

On the next episode, Adriana learns the truth.

Episode 8

Dr. Baker was sitting at his desk, looking at a picture of his three kids, Malik, Ivy, and Clay. It was a picture they took when they were teenagers. He realized he still hadn't heard anything from Ivy so he called her phone. No answer. He then called Malik. The phone rang.

Malik: Hey Dad.

Dr. Baker: Son, any word from Ivy?

Malik: No, still nothing. I was just about to call you.

Dr. Baker: What is it? Have you found out something?

Malik: Dad, what I'm about to tell you doesn't necessary mean anything okay.

Dr. Baker: What is it, Malik?

Malik: We found Ivy's car.

Dr. Baker: (Excited.) That's good news.

Malik: Dad, we found it at the bottom of a lake.

Dr. Baker's excitement quickly dropped. "My Lord."

Malik: We had forensic go through the car thoroughly. They found nothing, not a single fingerprint or anything.

Dr. Baker was silent. He didn't want to imagine the worst but he couldn't help it at this point.

Malik: Dad, you there?

Dr. Baker: Yes, son, I'm here. I have a bad feeling about this.

Malik: Dad, don't. I'm going to find her I promise.

Malik begin to think about what his mom told him before she died.

Malik: Mom told me that I was the oldest and I needed to look after Ivy and Clay. I promised her I will. I'm not going to break that promise now.

Dr. Baker: I know you won't, son.

Malik: Everyone here at the station is aware of what's going on. We're going to find her. Try not to worry. Okay?

Dr. Baker said "okay" but that still didn't wipe away the bad feeling he was having.

Malik: I will call you when I have more news.

Dr. Baker: Okay, son. Talk to you later.

They both hung up.

OUTSIDE THE HOSPITAL

Armon was standing outside, looking up at the stars when Adriana walked up behind him.

Adriana: Congratulations.

Armon turned around and said, "What do you want?"

Adriana: It's just so ironic how you keep hurting the ones you claim to love so much.

Armon: I don't have time to hear you rant. Why don't you just leave?

Adriana just stared at him then said, "No. You don't get it do you?"

Armon: Get what?

Adriana: Armon, my sister doesn't want you anymore. She has moved on. Why don't you just accept that.

Armon: Never.

Adriana: You are the reason Jase is in there fighting for his life right now. All because you can't accept the fact that Alexandria has moved on.

Armon stepped closer to Adriana.

Armon: I'm the reason? I'm not the one who pulled the trigger.

As soon as he said that Adriana slapped him. Armon moved toward her to grab her but caught himself. He was livid. Adriana didn't bulge.

Adriana: There it is. If only you could see the hate in your eyes right now. You want to grab me, don't you? Go ahead, Armon. Grab me. Slap me. That's what you like to do to my sister, isn't it?

Armon just stood there, staring at her.

Adriana: Like I always said, you are a pathetic excuse for a husband.

Armon: I am so sick of your self-righteous holier than thou ass. Let me tell you something since you think you have the perfect marriage and the perfect husband. Did Max tell you about the affair he had a week before you two was to get married? Huh? Did he tell you about the ten-year-old daughter he has because of that affair?

Adriana just laughed. "You would say anything right now want you? What make you think I will believe anything that comes out of your mouth?"

Armon: Because the woman who he had the affair with, and has his child, is my sister. His daughter, Ashley, is my niece. You don't have to believe me. When you ask him about it, which I know you will, his facial expression will tell you the truth.

Adriana was speechless. She had this blank look on her face.

Armon: Wait a minute, do you hear that?

Armon: (Looking around.) Silence. This is the first time I've known you to be without words. So tell me, who is the pathetic husband now?

Armon got in Adriana's face and looked her dead in the eyes and said, "Karma's a bitch, isn't she." Then he walked away leaving her outside. A single tear dropped from Adriana eye.

On the next episode, the mystery person continues to stalk Diane.

Episode 9

Brazil was at home resting before going back to the hospital. He was lying on the sofa when Ivan came from the backroom.

Ivan: Dad, is Mom coming to get me tonight?

Brazil sat up and looked at his son. "I don't know. How about I call your Uncle Malik and see if he has heard from her. He's a policeman."

Ivan: Yes, call him.

Brazil: Okay, you go back in the room, and I will call him now.

Ivan left and went back to the room to play. Brazil didn't have Malik's number so he had to call the police station. Phone rang.

Dispatch: Fulton County Police Department, how may I help you?

Brazil: Yes, do you have a police officer by the name of Malik there?

Dispatch: Yes, we do.

Brazil: Transfer me to him please.

Dispatch: Transferring now.

The dispatch transferred the call. Phone began to ring again.

Malik: This is Malik.

Brazil: Malik, hey, this is Brazil. Ivy's ex-husband.

Malik: Oh, hey, man.

Brazil: Have you heard anything?

Malik: No, I haven't. We did find her car, though.

Brazil: Really? Where was it?

Malik: It was behind an abandoned house at the bottom of a lake.

Brazil stood up. "What? Are you serious?"

Malik: Yes. We have everyone out looking for her and on alert. Let me ask you, do you know the last place she may have went?

Brazil: I'm not sure, but I think she mentioned something about going over to your house.

Malik: Okay, if you remember anything else call me. I will keep you posted as well.

Brazil: All right, thanks.

They both hung up.

MYSTERY'S HOUSE

Diane pulled in the driveway at Mystery's house. She was still staying there for the time being. Her mind was so preoccupied with everything that was going on; she didn't even notice she had been followed. The mystery person pulled off on the side of the road away from the house and cut the car off. He watched as Diane went inside. He got out of the car and walked behind the house. It was dark so he was certain he wouldn't be seen.

Diane locked the front door and went upstairs to the bedroom she was sleeping in. She got out fresh clothes to put on and laid them on the bed. She then went to the bathroom and turned on the shower to let the water run. As Diane undressed, steam from the hot water begin to fill the room. She stepped into the shower and let the water run all over her. She just closed her eyes. It felt like heaven.

The mystery person peeped inside a window. He was looking into the kitchen. The kitchen was dark because the light was off. He went to the back door and turned the knob. To his surprise, it was unlocked. He went inside and closed the door behind him. He walked quietly through the kitchen, picking up a butcher knife that was lying on the table. When he got to the stairs, he just stood there, looking up the staircase. He could hear water running. The mystery person proceeded up the stairs, scraping the walls with the knife. Halfway up, one of the stairs made a loud squeak as he stepped onto it. He came to a complete stop.

Diane opened her eyes. She thought she heard a noise. She cut off the shower for a second to see if she would hear it again. She heard nothing. She cut the shower back on and began to lather herself with soap.

The mystery person made it upstairs and went to the bathroom door. It was closed. He slowly opened it. Steam rushed out as the bathroom was completely filled with it. You could hardly see in front of yourself. He went inside the bathroom and over to the shower curtain. He grabbed the knife tighter as he rubbed his other hand across the curtain.

Diane was letting the water run all the soap off her at this point. She didn't want to get out the shower because it felt so good. She turned the water off and snatched back the shower curtains.

The mystery person was gone. She reached and grabbed a towel and began to dry herself off. She stepped out the shower and opened the door wide open so the steam could escape the bathroom. After she dried herself off, she went to her bedroom and got dressed. She then went downstairs to the kitchen. She turned on the kitchen light and jump. She was startled to see the back door was wide open. She closed it immediately and locked it. She couldn't imagine why it was left opened. She then thought to herself that maybe Mystery left if open in a rush. Confused, she proceeded to fix herself a sandwich. She hadn't eaten in days. She sat down and ate. As soon as she finished, she got her keys and left. As she backed out of the driveway and pulled off, the mystery person started his car and followed her back to the hospital.

On the next episode, Alexandria receives shocking news.

Episode 10

Melanie was sitting on her bed with her legs crossed Indian style. She had a small throw pillow in her lap and her scented candles burning. She loved scented candles and always kept two burning right beside her bed. The fragrance from the candles had her entire room smelling like fresh roses. Melanie was on the phone with Chris. They were so much in love with each other.

Melanie: So I was thinking.

Chris: What?

Melanie: How about you come back over tonight?

Chris: Are you sure?

Melanie: Yes.

Chris: That was kind of thrilling, sleeping over with you and your mom upstairs.

They both laughed.

Chris: What time you want me to come over?

Melanie: Around nine. We're fixing to head to the mall right now. I will leave the basement door unlocked for you that way if I'm not back you can wait for me inside. We should be back by then though.

Chris: Okay, sounds like a plan. I have something special for you too.

Melanie: What is it?

Chris started laughing. "You will see tonight."

Melanie: Tell me.

Chris: Nope.

Melanie: I hate when you do that to me.

Chris: But you love me, though.

They both laughed.

Malena called out from downstairs. "Melanie, let's go."

Melanie yelled back, "Okay, here I come."

Chris: You leaving now?

Melanie: Yes, so I will see you tonight.

Chris: You most certainly will. I love you.

Melanie: I love you too.

They hung up. Melanie jumped up and, not looking back, tossed the throw pillow back on the bed and ran out the door. Melanie, not even knowing, when she threw the pillow, she missed the bed, hitting the nightstand. The night stand shook, knocking over one of the candles. The candle hit the floor as it continued to burn. The fire from the candle caught the bottom of the curtains, and it started to burn.

Melanie made it downstairs. "I'm ready."

Malena: About time.

Malena, Melanie, and Ashley headed out the door. Malena locked the door behind her. She saw her neighbor out watering her flowers.

Malena: Hey, Barbara.

Barbara: Hey, how are you?

Malena: I'm well, thank you.

Malena and the girls got in the car and left for the mall.

At the Hospital

Dr. Walker came into the waiting room. Everyone stood up.

Alexandria: How is he, Doctor?

Dr. Walker: He is stable. We were able to remove the bullet from his chest. He's still not out of the woods yet. We have to run some more tests just to make sure there weren't any other damages. It will be a while before anyone can see him.

Everyone was relieved.

Dr. Walker: Alexandria, can you and your husband come with me to my office?

Alexandria and Armon both said "Sure."

Alexandria turned to Adriana.

Adriana: It's okay, go ahead. We're going to leave since Jase can't have any visitors right now. Call me if you need anything.

Alexandria: Thanks, sis.

Adriana and Max left.

When Alexandria and Armon got to Dr. Walker's office, he asked them both to have a seat.

Armon: Is there something wrong?

Dr. Walker: I didn't want to discuss this matter in front of everyone.

Alexandria: You're scaring me, Doctor.

Dr. Walker: Jase lost a tremendous amount of blood. We were unable to use either one your blood so we use what we had here in the hospital and call the local blood bank for the rest.

Alexandria: Wait a minute. What do you mean you were unable to use our blood?

Dr. Walker: Jase's blood type is O-, which means he can only receive O- blood. Alexandria, your blood type is AB+ and Armon is A+.

Alexandria: Dr. Walker what are you saying?

Dr. Walker: I'm sorry, Alexandria, but there is no way possible that you both together can be Jase's parents.

Alexandria: What?

On the next episode, Armon confesses the truth.

Episode 11

Diane made it back to the hospital. She went straight to Dr. Baker's office. When she got to his office, she knocked.

Dr. Baker: Come in.

Dr. Baker was sitting at his desk, looking over files when Diane walked in. He was happy to see her.

Diane: Hey, are you busy?

Dr. Baker stood up. "Of course not. Come on in." He went and greeted her with a hug and kiss. "You look refreshed."

Diane: (Jokingly.) Do I smell beter now?

Dr. Baker started laughing.

Diane: No, but seriously, I needed that shower. Thank you. You always seem to know what I need when I need it.

Dr. Baker: I'm a doctor, remember?

They both laughed.

Dr. Baker: Did you eat something?

Diane: I did.

Dr. Baker: That's my girl.

He gave her another hug.

Diane: Any change with Mystery?

Dr. Baker: Nope, he's still sleeping. I told you he would be.

There was another knock at the door.

Dr. Baker: (Sarcastically.) Just perfect. Come in.

Diane laughed. A nurse walked in.

Nurse: Dr. Baker, I have the DNA test results you requested.

Dr. Baker: Oh, great. Thank you.

The nurse handed over the results and left. The results were in a sealed envelope. Diane and Dr. Baker just stared at each other.

Dr. Baker: You still sure you want to go through with this?

Diane: Of course. I've waited over twenty something years for this.

Dr. Baker: Okay, before we open this, let me call and get Kennedy and Jackson back here. That way, I can give the results all at once.

Diane: Okay.

Dr. Baker sat down at his desk and made the calls.

MALIK'S HOUSE

The curtains in Melanie's room were now completely on fire. Smoke started to fill the room. The curtains dropped from the rod across the nightstand and onto the bed, catching the lamp shades on fire. The bed instantly caught fire because of the silk sheets. The fire spread quickly across the room. The entire room was now in flames and filled with smoke. The smoke started to escape the room into the hallway. The fire followed right behind it. The walls began to bubble up from the extreme heat. The wall paper started to peel back from the walls. Pictures shattered and fell to the floor. The fire continued to spread throughout the top level like someone had poured gasoline everywhere.

Barbara the neighbor was now watering her grass. All of a sudden, the windows blew out. Barbara jumped dropping the water hose.

Barbara: Oh my God.

Barbara ran into her house and call 911.

Dispatcher: 911, how may I help you?

Barbara: (Frantic.) Yes, my neighbor's house is on fire!

Dispatcher: Ma'am, is there anyone in the house.

Barbara: No, they're not home.

Dispatcher: What's the address?

Barbara: 1312 Hillcrest Lane.

Dispatch: Okay, I'm dispatching the fire department out now. They should be there in ten minutes.

Barbara: Okay, I need to call my neighbors.

Dispatch: Go ahead. Just keep a look out for the fire truck.

The fire continued to burn out of control. A crowd began to form outside to watch. More windows blew out. The top floor was completely engulfed. It was only a matter of time before the floor would collapse.

DR. WALKER'S OFFICE

Alexandria: What?

Dr. Walker: I'm so sorry.

Armon just dropped his head.

Alexandria: There's got to be some kind of mistake.

Dr. Walker: I personally ran each of your blood twice.

Alexandria: This can't be happening. What are we supposed to do?

Armon's head was still lowered.

Dr. Walker: I would suggest going back to the hospital where you gave birth and talking with the administration there. I don't know what procedures they would take you through, but that is the best place to start. Meanwhile I will continue to treat Jase as if he is your child.

Dr. Walker looked over at Armon then said, "I will give you both some time to talk. I'm going to go check on Jase."

Dr. Walker left the room. Alexandria stood up.

Alexandria: I can't believe this is happening. That is my son in there.

Alexandria started to cry.

Armon: Of course he is our son.

Armon got up and tried to comfort her by giving her a hug. She pushed him away.

Alexandria: (Yelling.) Get away from me. All of this is your fault. If you hadn't tried to attack me, none of this would be happening right now. Dr. Walker said Jase is not our child. Do you know what that means?

Armon: I heard what he said.

Alexandria: You just sat there with your head lowered. You acted like you weren't surprise by what he was saying. Your reaction was more like guilt, like you already knew.

Alexandria caught herself. She remembered that Armon was capable of anything.

Alexandria: Wait, did you already know?

Armon had this guilty defeated look on his face. "Alexandria."

Alexandria: (Yelling.) Answer me! Did you know?

Armon: Yes.

On the next episode, Ivy is scared for her life.

Episode 12

Armon: Yes, I already knew.

Alexandria: How could you keep something like that from me?

Armon: Alexandria, I didn't tell you because I didn't want to hurt you.

Alexandria: What do you mean you didn't want to hurt me? You knew I was raising someone else's child and you didn't think I had the right to know that?

Armon: You have to believe me when I tell you it was for your own sanity.

Alexandria: You are not even making sense right now. How long have you known about this?

Armon: (Taking a deep breath.) Since he was born.

Alexandria stared crying again. "Armon how could you? All this time? What happened to my own child?"

Armon: Let's not talk about that right now.

Alexandria getting angry got in his face. "We are going to talk about it." She shoved him. "What happened to my child?"

Armon: (Getting teary-eyed, yelled.) He died. Okay. He died.

MALIK'S HOUSE

Malena and the girls were sitting down eating. They had been in several stores and bought a lot of stuff. She always had a day out with the girls at least once a month. Malena phone rang. She pulled it out her pocketbook and saw it was her neighbor calling.

Malena answered, "Hey, Barbara."

Barbara: Malena, you need to get home now. Your house is on fire.

Malena: What? Oh my God. I'm on my way.

Malena hung up.

Melanie: Mom, what is it?

Malena: We need to go now. Our house is on fire.

They picked up their bags and ran out the mall to the car. Malena sped out of the parking lot.

Malena: Melanie, get your dad on the phone for me—hurry.

Melanie quickly called Malik and handed the phone to her mom.

Malik: Hello?

Malena: (Frantic.) Malik, where are you?

Malik could hear in her voice that something was wrong.

Malik: I'm on my way home. Is there something wrong?

Malena: Our house is on fire.

Malik: What? Are you and the girls okay?

Malena: Yes, we were at the mall. We're on our way but it will be about fifteen minutes before we get there.

Malik: I'm five minutes out. I'll be pulling up any second.

Malena: Just be careful when you get there.

They hung up. Malik put his police flashers on and sped home. As he got closer, he could see smoke in the air. When he pulled up, he saw the fire truck and firemen there spraying water into and on top of his house. He jumped out of the car and ran up. One of the firemen caught him but recognized he was in uniform.

Fireman: Officer, you can't go any closer. The house is unstable.

Malik: That is my house.

Fireman: Was there anyone home?

Malik: No, my wife and kids are out.

As soon as Malik said that, the entire top floor collapsed onto the main level. Malik watched in shock.

Ivy heard and felt the rumble from the floor collapsing. She looked up at the ceiling, wondering what that could have been. Minutes later, she noticed smoke entering the storage room from under the door. She realized to herself that the house must be on fire. She began to scream but couldn't. The tape around her mouth was smothering the sound. She continued to scream anyway. She thought to herself, *I can't die down here*. She continued to struggle to get free but couldn't.

On the season finale, we all want to know "Whose the father?"

Episode 13

Max and Adriana had made it back to the hotel room. Max noticed something was bothering Adriana.

Max: Hey, babe, are you okay? You didn't say one word all the way here.

Adriana: (Bluntly.) I'm fine.

Max: Are you sure because—

Adriana interrupted him, "I said I'm fine."

Max was surprised by her reaction. "Whoa, whoa, what's the matter? Why are you so hostile right now?"

Adriana: I'm not hostile. I'm just frustrated and angry right now.

Max: Is it Jase? Because believe me, I share your feeling. I want him to get better just as much as you.

Adriana: It's not Jase.

Max: Well, what's got you so angry?

Adriana: It's something that Armon said.

Max: Are you serious right now? You have never let anything that Armon said upset you or get to you like this. You know how he likes to get under our skin.

Adriana: Max, I'm going to ask you something, and I want you to be honest with me.

Max: Sure, anything.

Adriana closed her eyes and took a deep breath.

Max: What is it?

Adriana looked dead in his face and said, "Who is Ashley?"

Dr. Walker's Office

Alexandria: (Crying.) My baby died?

Armon: Yes. Now you see why I didn't want you to know.

Alexandria: What happened to him?

Armon: The details are not important.

Alexandria: This is my child we're talking about. Everything is important. Now tell me what happened to him.

Armon: The nurse at that time called it SIDS.

Alexandria: SIDS? What is that?

Armon: It's short for Sudden Infant Death Syndrome. It's a term doctors use when a perfectly healthy baby dies while sleeping. There's no cause for it known to date. It's something that just happens.

Alexandria put her hands over her mouth. "Did he suffer?"

Armon: No. He fell asleep in my arms and never woke up.

Alexandria: My poor baby.

Armon: I was devastated. I wasn't about to let you go through that.

Alexandria: So what did you do, because I took a newborn baby home from the hospital?

Armon didn't say anything.

Alexandria: What did you do, Armon? I have a right to know.

Armon: Okay, I will tell you the whole truth. But know this, everything I did, I did because I loved you. I never wanted you to find out this way.

Alexandria: Just tell me.

Armon: The day after you gave birth, I was in the babies' nursery ward holding our son. He was perfectly fine. I couldn't keep my eyes off him. He was sleeping so peacefully in my arms. He was our first child, and I was a proud father. I was in there for about an hour. When the nurse came and took him from me, she noticed he wasn't breathing. She worked on him and did all she could to revive him right there in front of me. He just wouldn't take a breath. I was going out of my mind. Before she called it in, I stopped her.

Alexandria: What do you mean you stopped her?

Armon didn't want to go on.

Alexandria: Armon? What do you mean?

Armon: I bribed her to help me.

Alexandria: To help you do what?

Armon: Switch the babies and to never tell anyone.

Alexandria put her hands over her mouth. "You switched our dead child with someone else's baby?

Armon: Yes.

Alexandria: And she didn't tell anyone?

Armon: No. I paid her a lot of money to keep quiet and to resign. It wasn't easy, but she finally agreed.

Alexandria: You're lying. You didn't bribe her. You threatened her into helping you, didn't you?

Armon: I did what I had to do to keep you happy.

Alexandria: No, you did this for yourself. Whose child did you switch our baby with?

Armon: I don't know. A newborn had just come in a few hours before our baby died.

Alexandria: You're lying again.

Armon: Just drop it. You know the whole truth. Now let's just focus on Jase.

Alexandria: No, there is something you're not telling me. What is it?

Alexandria got the thinking back to when she gave birth.

Alexandria: Wait a minute. There was only one other person that gave birth around the same time I did and in the same hospital.

Armon: Alexandria, stop. Don't go there.

Alexandria continued to run that time through her head. She remembered. Alexandria looked at Armon and started to cry.

Alexandria: Oh my God, no. Armon, you didn't. It's Adriana. She's Jase's mother, isn't she?

MALIK'S HOUSE

Malena pulled up. She had to park further back because the fire department had roped the area off with caution tape. On top of that, there was now a huge crowd watching. She switched the car off. She and the girls jumped out and ran toward the caution tape.

Ashley: Mom, there's dad. Dad? Dad?

Malik turned around and all three ran into his arms. He kissed them all.

Malik: I'm so glad you're all safe.

Malena just covered her mouth and started to cry. Then Melanie and Ashley started to cry as they held onto their dad.

The fire was still burning ferociously. It seemed the water that the firemen were spraying wasn't helping. All of a sudden, there was an explosion. Everyone, including the crowd, backed away. The fire had gotten to the water heater, which caused the explosion. The main level of the house collapsed into the basement.

Malena thought about Ivy.

Malena: Oh my God.

The fireman ran back to Malik. "There's nothing else we can do. We will continue with the water but the fire may have to burn itself out. Are you sure no one else was in that house.?"

Malik: Yes, I'm sure.

Malena blurted out, "No."

They all stopped and looked at Malena.

Malik: Malena, what do you mean no? Is there someone else in there?

Malena was nervous and scared. She just stood there froze.

Malik yelled, "Malena, who else is in that house?"

Malena: (Crying.) Malik . . . Ivy's in there.

Malik: What?

DR. BAKER'S OFFICE

Dr. Baker and Diane were talking when there was a knock at the door.

Dr. Baker: Come in.

Jackson walked in. "Hey." He saw that Kennedy wasn't there. "Where's Kennedy?"

Dr. Baker: He should be here any minute.

Jackson: Good, because I'm ready to get this over with.

Diane rolled her eyes. There was another knock.

Dr. Baker: Come on in, Ken.

Kennedy walked in.

Dr. Baker: Okay, we all know why we are here. To find out who is the father of Diane's sons, Mystery and Brazil. Being that Mystery and Brazil are identical twins, I only had to use Mystery's DNA and blood sample since he is here in the hospital. As you can see, the envelope is sealed. I will be learning the results for the first time as well as you.

Dr. Baker took a letter opener from his desk and opened the envelope. He removed the letter inside and started to read.

Dr. Baker: This letter is to inform you of the paternity results of Subject A, which is Mystery. Biological specimens corresponding to Subject A Mystery were submitted along with biological specimens from Alleged Father 1, which is you, Kennedy, and biological specimens from Alleged Father 2, which is you, Jackson.

Kennedy: Joshua, it's just us here. Can we just hear the results please?

Diane: I agree. This anticipation is killing me.

Dr. Baker: Okay. Let me skip down to the conclusion. Okay, based on evidence of DNA analysis, it is confirmed that the biological father for Subject A is . . .

Dr. Baker hesitated.

Diane: Joshua, who is it? Who is the father?

Dr. Baker lifted his head and said, "It's you."

To be continued.

About the Author

Shawn Pierce was born and raised in Georgia. He is a graduate of Georgia Southern University with a BBA in Accounting. Shawn currently resides in Atlanta where he works as a cost control engineer. He also owns his own trucking company called Pierce Trucking. Shawn has always been interested in screenplays and writing so he finally took the chance to explore it and published his first book, *Mystery*, back in 2015.

Now the new sequel, *Mystery Book 2* brings back the drama and suspense like never before.

CPSIA information can be obtained
at www.ICGtesting.com
Printed in the USA
FFOW03n0029231217
44170675-43569FF

9 781640 826847